Fanny's Flight

Rita Traut Kabeto

Rita Traut Kabeto

Fanny's Flight

ISBN 978-0-557-41370-6

Fanny's Flight

When I graduated from the convent boarding school during the mid 1950s, Germany was still under the occupation of the victorious Allies. They dictated policy in the country much as my Mother dictated policy at home. Mother was a big, stout woman, taller than Father, and large-boned, with big breasts and big buttocks, all of it encased in a corset that kept her various body parts stiff, tight, and unresponsive. There was nothing soft about Mother. She prided herself in never wearing make-up and never cutting her brown hair. She wore it straight back out of her face, braided into one thick, long braid that she wrapped into a knot at the nape of her neck.

I had no idea what was going to happen with me. I was fifteen, and that seemed to be the end of things. My parents never talked about my future, never told me of their plans for me, if they had any. From day to day I was told to do this or that, here or there, this way or that way. Nothing regular, nothing consistent, like facing a wall and not knowing what was behind it. Neither Father nor Mother ever asked me what I wanted or liked to do. As a consequence, whatever faint, shadowy dreams for the future I might have had as a child never grew to reach my consciousness. I had no dreams.

Mother could never keep a housemaid for very long. She called them sloppy and undisciplined; they called her picky and demanding. During World War II, when Germany was the occupier in Russia, our housemaids were young countrywomen from Poland and Russia who had been transported against their will to Germany to work in the war effort. But my parents were allowed to have a Russian maid because of our large family. After the war, however, Mother had to select among local young women who were better educated and increasingly conscious of their rights. When Mother lost another housemaid she thought it a waste of time to look for a replacement since they never could do anything right anyway. She decided that I could fill the bill. Beside business courses I had also learned cooking, housekeeping and infant care. Father said nothing about it. I was never asked.

That summer was not a happy time. My eldest sister, Erna, had died in a traffic accident the year before and the wounds, untreated and unhealed beneath thin scars, erupted painfully from time to time. My second eldest sister, Paula, after waiting out a respectable but impatiently endured mourning period, had recently been married. Eighteen-year-old Walter, crown prince of family and business assets, had the freedom to come and go as he pleased. He was soon to leave for work in Munich. That left me, Stephanie Sauerling, as the oldest one to look after Hans, Hildegard, Markus and Matthias.

"When do I get to work in the office?" I asked innocently one Saturday. I was stirring the potato soup while Mother had just finished with the big sheet cake.

"Take the cake to the bakery now," replied Mother. I carried that big awkward thing, too wide and long for our own oven, with one long side shelved on my hip and the other long side held by my hand on an angled arm. I would have to pick it up before the bakery closed.

Through a strange twist of nature, Mother was born and reared on a farm, yet she intensely disliked animals. She preferred working in our store, which was located on the street level of our house, a four-story downtown building that stood at the corner of two busy streets and ran along each one in equal parts. She basked in the adulation of local housewives who admired her eightfold motherhood status and esteemed her for being a capable businesswoman as well. She didn't spend much time in the kitchen other than putting finishing touches on dinners so that Father, who was very picky, would not have an excuse to pout. Once in a while, though, something came over her and then she made noodles from scratch.

It took a while, but eventually I realized that I had become a permanent housemaid. And every minute not occupied with household chores I spent looking after my younger siblings. Hans was thirteen, quiet, introspective, a tinkerer who lived in his own little world. He was only troublesome at bedtime when I had to coax him out of his secret realm into domestic reality. Hildegard, a sweet girl of ten, could be a lot of trouble. She had loved Erna dearly, and her sudden death had traumatized Hildi. Her grades had suffered; she had become withdrawn and obstinate when she didn't want to do as I told her. Mother was no help; when in a good mood she had the patience of a cat at the mouse hole and coddled Hildegard; when in a bad mood she slapped her around. Markus was in second grade, Matthias in first. They were like twins in body size and did everything together. On the one hand, they were part of the reason why I was stuck in the role of mother; on the other hand, I was glad to have them because they occasioned my only fun - sledding and ice skating in winter, swimming in summer.

"You know, Mother, I would really like to go out tomorrow afternoon," I told her one Saturday after lunch. Mother looked at me, puzzled.

"Out where?" she said.

"I don't know yet. Just out."

"That's the strangest thing I ever heard," she answered and shook her head.

"I just want to be by myself for a little while. I look after the kids all day, I do all the housework – I need a little time off."

"Time off?" she said with a look of astonishment. "Doing what? There's work to be done."

"I need a little time to myself. Time to think, maybe go for a walk, or to a movie, or just sit on the park bench for a while."

"Sit on a park bench for a while? That's what cats do not respectable young girls. What would people think to see you sitting on a park bench by yourself. It's out of the question."

"Well how about just going to a movie," I said in desperation.

"Well, okay. If it's a family type movie you can take the kids with you," she replied

The days passed in irksome monotony. Housework, cooking, babysitting, housework, cooking, babysitting, housework, cooking, babysitting... I could never go anywhere – not that I had a girl friend to go with. Three years in boarding school out of town had severed connections with girls my own age at home, and Mother's controlling influence prevented any nurturing of new connections. Even going to a movie was difficult because I could not leave until the kids were in bed, and, since they seldom stayed put, babysitting often drew out endlessly. Occasionally, I even missed choir practice, something that Mother approved of as a pious, churchy activity. What's more, our choir director had a Ph.D. in music, and all educated people – men, by nature – were to be esteemed and obeyed. That this divorced man also had a lecherous giggle, Mother never knew.

Every German housemaid had at least one day off per week, had certain rights and, of course, income. I had nothing. What little pocket money I received from Father once per month I turned into chocolate and candy. There was never anything left for such things as nylons, or new clothes. Supposedly, Mother and Father would provide my clothes, but Mother's ideas of what I needed fell way short of reality. On any given Sunday I had exactly one pair of nylons to wear, so that I was plagued by constant fear that my stockings might develop a run during morning mass and then embarrass me at evening prayer services.

"I need an extra pair of nylons, Mother, but I don't have any money," I told her on another occasion.

"You have a pair, don't you?"

"Yes, but if they get a run I have nothing else to wear."

"So you take them off after church, and then they'll be good for prayer service in the evening."

"Mother, I do all the work around here. Can't I have an extra pair of nylons?"

"Where do you think the money is coming from?"

"I need some nylons," I insisted, and my voice began to teeter on the verge of panic.

"Get to work," she said in measured tones, her eyes wide and harsh.

How I wished Steffi could visit again. She was my girlfriend from the boarding school in Venusbrunn who had the same name as I. We had managed to avoid confusion by calling her Steffi, and I was called Stef. Steffi lived in Wiesenthal, not very far from Hanfurt. I wished she could come again, but there was no point in asking Mother. After all, who would look after the kids and do the work if I had company. But what was worse, Steffi and I had been blamed for causing Erna's death. In a vision, Steffi had seen Erna getting hit by a car, and she had felt the need to stop it. We had hatched a plan that was successful, but Erna hag gotten so angry with us for manipulating her that she left the house in a big huff. Being so very upset probably made her careless when crossing the street. That's when she got hit by a car and died. –

For a year and a half I did as I was told, never selfish, always helpful and mindful of my duties, yet Mother never seemed to notice. Obedience was a highly regarded Christian virtue, and it was preached to us from the pulpit, through lessons, and by every adult. In that vein, wanting anything for oneself was being selfish, and selfishness was the ultimate evil. But evil or not, my inner person began nagging that it needed, or wanted something. I became restless.

"Can I take dancing lessons?" I asked Mother one day. Both Erna and Paula had gone to dancing school. It was an important social event for young people in Hanfurt, and the course usually ended with a grand ball.

"I have to think about it," Mother said as she hurried for the door to go downstairs to meet her adoring customers. Waiting on them and receiving their respect made her happy, although such happiness usually evaporated on her way upstairs. When I didn't hear any more about dancing, I reminded her.

"I'll have to talk to your Father about it."

"What's there to talk about?" I said impatiently. "Erna and Paula took lessons when they were sixteen. I'm almost eighteen. Shouldn't it be my turn now?"

"I will tell you when it's your turn," she said in a sharp tone, her dark piercing eyes sending shock waves through my system.

I waited another week, then I brought it up again, timidly, and fearful of the reaction. That my timid approach could produce precisely that which I feared didn't occur to me until much later.

"It's not right for a young girl to go out after dark," she blurted out, irritated, annoyed at me for not letting her forget it. "What will people think to see you walking the street alone at night!" Mother, the country bumpkin, feared the opinion of the city dwellers that she considered to be high above her own native station because some of them had gone to school a little longer than the minimum eight years.

"Well, maybe Dad could pick me up after class," I suggested gingerly.

"It's out of the question," she answered so highly indignant as if I had asked that Father pick me up in Dneprovskaya, Russia.

"Or Paula?"

"You can ask her," Mother said.

I called Paula and told her of my dilemma. She agreed to do it. I told Mother. Mother said she would get back with Paula. When I heard no more about it, I went to speak with Paula in person. She lived a few minutes walk away in the old part of town near our parish church. She was helping with a customer in her husband's photo shop when I came in. I watched her sales demeanor and thought it was quite professional. She had had plenty of experience during the years that she spent in Father's business. Paula had always been called the prettiest of us girls by Father's male employees. Some of them were so thoughtless as to say it directly to my face, causing me feelings of envy and inadequacy.

Paula seemed to be nervous, and perhaps even intimidated by her husband who kept watch over her even while waiting on another customer. From time to time Werner looked at me, a most peculiar look that made me quite uncomfortable. I would have been alarmed had I not been reared to believe that all businessmen who owned a store were, therefore, morally upright and decent people. Werner had straight, dark brown hair and an olive complexion. His thick lips, which might have been sensuous, gave an impression of cruelty instead. I decided to wait outside till Paula was done.

When she was finished she took me to her apartment beside the shop. It was actually a separate but connected little house in a row of several two or three story elderly homes that had begun to sag into each other over the centuries. "Just call me if you need me," she called back to her husband. She was chewing gum, gnashing it with a vengeance as if she was trying to cripple it for life. Father called it a nasty habit that had infiltrated German culture and society with the advent of the American occupation. Cows chewing their cud, he would remark with utter derision. We kids thought it was cool.

"You're nervous," I said, part statement, part question.

"You could tell, huh. Werner makes me nervous. So I chew. It's better and easier than smoking. So, how are the dance classes going? Do you have a nice partner?"

"Nothing of the sort. I haven't even begun. Mother said she'd have to discuss it with you first. Did she call you about it?"

"No, she hasn't," Paula said.

"What's the matter with her?" I whined. "Why won't she let me have lessons?"

"She'll have to buy you a new dress, and shoes probably, too," said Paula with a short laugh that signified intimate knowledge of the problem and, at the same time relief that it was now someone else's pain instead of hers. "You know how she is. She tried hard to talk Erna and me out of new clothes, too. But we kept bugging her until we got them."

Having that talk with Paula made me regret ever having wished Erna dead. Hateful as she had been to me, I wished that she were still around. Perhaps together, my two big sisters could do things for me. As it was, I felt terribly alone.

Then I had a brilliant idea. I said to Mother, "you don't even have to buy me a new dress for dancing lessons. I'm sure Paula would let me wear hers."

"Well, all right," Mother said absentmindedly. I could have jumped for joy, yet feared that she might change her mind once she realized that she had given her consent while her mind was occupied otherwise.

On a mild and fragrant spring day in May I went to my first class. I wore my Sunday dress, which was made from a material that Mother had taken away from Paula as punishment for something she had done. On a white background, it had large balloon-shaped dots in reds and blues. It had a simple fitted bodice with just a hint of sleeves, but the best part was a hugely flared skirt. I showed it off with the use of several layers of formerly stiff but now wilted petticoats. I was slender and well proportioned. In this dress I felt like a million. I tied my straight blond hair, which I had never been permitted to cut, like a ponytail, then slipped it through and wrapped it around a contraption that looked like a sausage ring into a large knot. Several large hairpins held it in place high on the back of my head. Skimpy flat shoes that minimized my large feet completed my outfit. I relished a rare sense of being attractive.

Classes were held in the grand hall of the Orangerie, a separate building but part of the city castle. It had once been the home of the princes of Hessen but was now occupied by city and state government agencies, except for the Orangerie with its large halls that were used for balls, dance classes, citywide parties, dignitary receptions, and similar events.

On the very first day, our instructor, an over-the-hill ex-ballet dancer, paired me up with a young man named Leon. He was just a little taller than I and had thick, wavy blond hair that stood straight up at the forehead. It reminded me of Erna who had the same thick, wavy hair that stood straight up at the forehead. Leon was clumsy. He kept stepping on my feet, couldn't get the hang of the waltz rhythm, apologized profusely and seemed awfully nervous. During breaks I tried to get away from him, but it was useless. He seemed to think we were matched for life. I went home alone that night. Mother didn't seem to care.

For some inexplicable reason, I found myself thinking often about Leon and actually looked forward to seeing him again. I even experienced a slight case of butterflies on the following Wednesday. Leon arrived first. As soon as he saw me he came over to me and greeted me with a shy smile. His hands were clammy and he was nervous again. To ease the tension – his and mine – I asked him what kind of work he did for a living.

"I'm a butcher, a journeyman butcher." he replied.

I didn't think much of butchers. They kill animals. Of course, they also provide good meat and sausages to eat. But they kill animals. Leon didn't say any more about it. I told him a few things about my large family. I wasn't used to talking much. Then Leon told me about his even larger one, and how they had fled their home in the East before the oncoming Russians and Poles at the end of the World War II. His family lived now in a small town outside of Hanfurt.

"Where do you work?" he asked me.

"In my Father's business," I replied, not wanting to tell him that I was stuck in the menial position of housemaid. "And you?"

"At Brandt's butchery," he answered. "I live there, too. The boss and I share a small room above the shop. He isn't married, you know. Their house is over four hundred years old," he added, at which point he lost count of the waltz we were practicing and stepped on my foot.

It must be a skewed and lumpy old thing like Paula's house, I thought, at which point I lost count of the waltz we were practicing and stepped on his foot. Our apologies happened simultaneously. We laughed.

"We better talk later, during the break," he suggested.

When class was over he asked to walk me home. He offered me his arm, and I put mine in his and we walked politely like a couple - like two people in a relationship. It made me feel almost dizzy with excitement to see myself in that role. I had seen it exhibited by other young people, had

9

longed to experience it for myself, yet without any hope that I ever would.

It had grown dark and few people were out and about. We were too shy to say much. It was a short walk to my house. When we reached it, he said he'd wait until I was safely inside. The outer building door was already locked. Now I had to ring the bell and wait for Mother to appear at the window on the third floor. She would check to see who was ringing, pull back her head, get the great bundle of keys that included the building key, then throw it down to me, wrapped in a towel which unraveled on the way down, and looked like a rumpled bomb descending on me.

"We're not allowed to have a key," I said in explanation. I was embarrassed, but Leon just smiled politely.

"See you next Wednesday," he said, but suddenly added, "if not before. Maybe you could come by the butcher shop sometime, during the week."

"We usually shop at Winter's butchery," I answered.

"Well, good night then," he said and turned to leave.

"Who was that man with you," Mother asked as I entered the apartment. She had been waiting by the door, and in order to better see me she had turned on the light above it, the only light in the house, it seemed to me, that had power enough to reveal things.

"With me? I don't know. Nobody. Just somebody walking past, I guess." Mother's piercing eyes scrutinized my face, but she said no more.

I could hardly wait for Wednesday to arrive again, and when it finally did, my stomach was churning with excitement. I couldn't figure out why. Leon still had that same thick curly hair that stood straight up at the forehead just like Erna's. He was still clumsy and stepped on my foot now and then. His hands still got clammy, and he was still nervous, but he listened to me. He not only listened, he was truly interested in what I had to say. At first, I didn't know what to say, as if lack of practice had plugged up the connection between thought and words. By the time the third class rolled around, though, it came out of me as if a faucet had suddenly been turned on. I talked about Venusbrunn, my favorite place in all the world, to which I was more drawn than my own hometown. Leon talked about his family's escape from the Eastern region, which had been part of Germany before World War II. It was a fascinating story of real hardship and deprivation.

Reaching my house but not finished with talking, we kept walking down the street to the next corner, turned around and came back, went down the street again, turned and came back. The clock on the nearby Protestant church rang half past ten - high time to get home. Leon made himself invisible by leaning against the house wall so that Mother couldn't see him when she threw down the bomb.

"Where have you been?" she asked, and her face was not friendly.

"At the class," I said, trying very hard to sound casual while shaking inwardly.

"Till now?" she asked, her tone severe, her piercing eyes searching my face for telltale signs of lying or worse.

"Well, it got a little later than usual. Teacher was spending more time with one of the guys who's a bit clumsy. We thought we'd watch."

"We? Who is we?"

"Well, the rest of the class." Mother let it go. She joined Father in the living room to watch the late news on television. I got ready for bed, then poked my head through a gap in the living room door and simply threw a "good night" into the general direction of my parents. I hadn't felt like kissing them for a long time.

On the following Saturday, I went to Brandt's butchery to buy the meat for Sunday dinner. It was farther away than the place where we usually shopped, so I had to hurry. While the counter help went to cut the meat that Mother wanted, I spied Leon through the large window in the door that led to the back of the shop. He wore a white uniform with light blue stripes,

11

almost like a jailbird, I thought. He didn't see me, though, and I was disappointed for not having had a chance to talk with him. But it was just as well, because the butchery was full of women shoppers. Some of them could well know me. One could never keep a secret in Hanfurt.

When Wednesday rolled around again, I had a hard time getting away from Hildegard. The little boys were ready for bed, Hans was still reading, but Hildegard, who shared a room with me, clung to me to keep me from leaving. "Fannie, tell me about Erna again," she whined. She always wanted to know about Erna, that she was dead, why she was dead, would she come back again, when would she come back again. It was bad enough to have my guilty conscience aroused every time I heard the name Erna, but to talk about the incident in detail was agony for me.

"I've told you a hundred times," I said sternly.

"Tell me again. Tell me what happened," she whined more insistently. I looked at my watch. It was time to leave for class. I couldn't bear to be late; I feared that Leon might get paired up with some other girl.

"Ask Mom or Dad," I said.

"They don't want to talk about Erna," she complained.

"Yeah, I know. Probably hurts too much," I replied. Yet Hildegard wanted to talk about Erna. It actually made her happy to talk and hear about Erna. It was not surprising, really, because talking about Erna was all that Hildegard had left of her. Yet Mother and Father preferred silence.

"I know what we can do," I said and went to get Hans. He was engrossed in a book about the universe. "Hans, do me a favor and talk to Hildi about Erna. I've got to get to class."

"What's there to say?" Hans replied.

"Anything, really. As long as you talk about Erna Hildi is happy; it doesn't matter much what you say. Besides, you have a great imagination. You'll think of something, huh?"

"Oh, all right," he said, put his book aside and got comfortable on my bed. Then he faced Hildegard who had grabbed her two favorite stuffed animals, a small black teddy that had leaked much of its stuffing, and a white seal that had turned gray with time and loving. They were wrapped into what had once been a baby blanket but was now just a rag. She held the grayish, ragged bundle close to herself and settled down in the corner of her bed.

"O.K.?" I asked. Hildi smiled and nodded. I left the room, and then stopped for a moment to listen to what Hans might be dreaming up.

"Once upon a time, in the far away region of Galactica, way past millions of unknown planets and stars, there lived a princess named Hildegard who had a big sister named Erna…" I peeked through the door; Hans's face had taken on a look of mystery, and Hildegard, all smiles, listened intently.

While Father was watching the early evening news on television, Mother was fixing him a cold supper in the kitchen. I opened the door, stuck my head through the gap and said, "I'm leaving now. Can I take the house key with me?"

"No," said Mother. "You just ring the bell."

With Erna fresh on my mind, I told Leon how Steffi had seen Erna die in one of her visions, and how we had plotted to save her. Actually, Steffi had plotted; I would have loved to get rid of Erna, whom I hated, and who hated me. But Steffi wouldn't let me. So we plotted, and we succeeded, but Erna died anyway. Sometimes, in an unguarded moment, the awful thought popped into my head that Erna might have died precisely because we tried to prevent her death. Had we left her alone, she would not have gotten so angry with us and might have been more careful when she crossed the street. The one thing that Father had taught us, had drilled into us since we were old enough to walk was how to cross the street safely. We always obeyed because we knew he'd be watching us from an upstairs window.

Leon, in his kind and patient way, listened quietly as I poured out my heart to him. We were walking arm-in-arm, with him next to the pavement for protection of the lady, as we had learned during the etiquette part of dancing class. "You shouldn't feel so guilty," he said. "You were trying to help. Your intentions were good; that counts for something. Who knows, maybe your sister died not because you meddled in her life, but despite your meddling. Because it was meant to be."

"Yeah, I know. I just wish I could stop feeling guilty."

"You will, in time," Leon assured me and he put his arm around me in a loving, protective way.

"That's what Judith said, too. She's a lady I met in Wiesenthal where Steffi lives. Steffi is psychic, you know, and Judith helps her make sense of the visions she has, and what she should do – or not do." A grin spread across Leon's face.

We had walked past the house once and I began to feel uneasy. "I better get home," I said and turned back.

"Lets go to a movie some time," Leon remarked suddenly.

"Yes, let's do that, " I said and began thinking about a way to accomplish it. I could dream up all sorts of plans, but I could never be sure from one day to the next if I would be free to carry them out. Leon was free to come and go as he pleased outside of his work hours. I was tied down like a housewife and mother with four children, but without any of the privileges that married status conferred upon a woman.

Before the next Sunday rolled around, I asked Mother if I could go to a movie on Sunday afternoon. "If you take your Father with you," she said. That was the queerest thing I had ever heard her say. My parents never went to a movie. Never. Father spent his Sunday afternoons in his office on the second floor, at least until he felt like going for a drive. And that always led him first to the warehouse where he checked to see that everything was as it should be: that the gate to the loading yard was locked, that all the lights were out, that no vandalism had occurred. Father going to a movie? Never.

I figured it was a ruse to prevent me from going as well. I went by Leon's butchery and let him know that he should meet me at the theater at three o'clock. I chose the one that was located in an opposite direction from our warehouse. I sneaked out of the apartment around two-thirty, didn't shut the door to keep from making a noise that would have alerted Mother. The downstairs door to the building was unlocked in the daytime.

"You made it," said Leon, and his broad smile was a sure sign of his pleasure to see me.

"I sneaked out of the house," I explained. "I'm a little worried about the reception when I get back, though."

"Why didn't you just tell your Mother that you wanted to go to a movie," he asked.

"Because she always says no."

"Always?" he asked.

"Yes, always. Now if I ask and she says no, and then I leave anyway, that's much worse than just sneaking out without a word," I explained.

"You have to learn to stand up for yourself," he said simply.

"I know, I know. Some day I'll have to do that. But right now is not the right time."

"Why not?"

"Oh, you have to know my Mother to understand," I said. Leon bought the tickets and we went inside. It was GONE WITH THE WIND and lasted three hours instead of the usual two. It was lovely to sit with Leon by my side, hand in hand, no Mother or Father looking over my shoulder. Once two hours had passed, though, I began to fidget impatiently. I grew worried over the length of my absence. On my way home the worry turned to fear, and even Leon could not talk me into relaxing. But I was lucky. My sister Paula and her husband Werner had come and were staying for supper. Mother would never scold me or yell at me or – heaven forbid – give the broomstick a workout on me in front of company. Instead, she

15

put on her best face - a very formal, polite, and sickly-sweet smile, had her brown eyes especially wide open, because she believed them to be her best feature. By the time I had put the kids to bed and Paula and Werner had left, it was time for me to go to bed as well.

Walter told me next day that he had seen me with Leon. I made him promise not to tell. "Why not?" he asked teasingly.

"Because I don't want Mother to know."

"Why not? You're not going to be a nun are you?"

"No, of course not," I said and laughed. "But don't tell her anyway, okay?"

"Does Mother want you to be a nun?" he asked.

"Wally, you know how she is – always saying no to everything. Come to think of it - no, you don't know how she is. You're not a girl. She's different with you. You can come and go as you like. If you need to, you can always pretend to have something to do in the office or the warehouse. Me, she always wants at home, all the time."

"That's because you're her favorite," he snickered.

"Oh sure, her favorite house and nurse maid."

"Of course! If you weren't around she'd have to do all the work. See? So you really are her favorite," he said and laughed again.

"Oh, now I see! She's tired of being the housewife, so she makes me do it. She'd much rather wait on customers and play the great Frau Sauerling who manages such a large household, and works in the store, and even grows a large garden. Such a hard worker! Such a devoted Mother! Such a capable business woman!" I began to feel real fear, because I suddenly saw myself stuck in the role of substitute mother and housewife forever.

I had to get out of it. But what to do? How would I even start? I would never be allowed to simply go out looking for a job. Mother thought it degrading to clean up other people's dirt. She had done it for many years before Father married her.

But working in Father's office was not the same as cleaning up after other people; she couldn't object to that.

One evening, when I knew Father to be alone in his office on the second floor, I went downstairs to talk to him. It had always been difficult, if not impossible, to talk to him about personal matters. Business problems never unhinged him, but with personal matters he came unglued. His face would wrinkle up in annoyed irritation, his hand would distractedly pat his bald head, and his body would twist and turn as though trying to get away from something unpleasant. It was enough to make one want to give up before even trying. I had to make a move, though. I dreaded the encounter.

"Dad, I need to talk to you," I said. Father was sitting at his desk, his pen propped horizontally in his mouth. It was a warm day and he had taken off his jacket. He looked at me for a moment. His broad face wrinkled up in irritated folds, the end of his long nose reached for his mouth as if to see what was coming out of it. He began to fidget, pulled on his suspenders, then stood up. I felt like running right there and then, but forced myself to stay put. "I've gone to business school and now I want to work in the office before I forget everything I learned."

"Your Mother needs you at home," he said lamely, no longer looking at me. His hand searched out his meager gray hair ring around his bald head.

"She can hire someone else," I replied, and my voice became shrill with the fear of losing my battle before it had begun. "Besides, didn't you send me to Venusbrunn to learn typing, and shorthand, and bookkeeping and all that? And what for? So that I forget it all in the kitchen?"

"I'll talk to Mother about it," he said reluctantly as he sat down again. I didn't dare say any more and hightailed it out of there.

I felt good about having confronted Father, but I feared it would be a long struggle and probably end with no change. Father would claim that he hadn't had a chance to talk to

Mother. Then Mother would claim that she hadn't had a chance to think about it. Then each would say they agree if the other agreed, and they would never come together on it. I knew the scenario. It was awful.

For the first time, I told Leon about how things really stood with me and my so-called job. We walked up and down the street a long time that night. I was full of myself and my problems and didn't realize how late it was getting. When the church clock struck eleven, I panicked.

Mother said nothing when I came in. Her mouth was set tight; she turned immediately and headed for the kitchen. I knew what was coming and managed to slip into the bathroom, the only room in the house that had a key in its lock, before she came after me with the big wooden spoon. There was nothing else for her to do but rant and rage through the door and accuse me of roaming the streets like a bitch in heat. I had saved myself, and I had prevented another wooden cooking spoon from needing replacement.

The atmosphere at home grew heavy. What little friendly conversation had existed between Mother and me stopped altogether. When the next dancing class came around, she warned me to be home by nine-thirty sharp or else.

My seventeenth birthday was only two weeks away. Mother never made much of birthdays. Father was more sentimental. He would round us up early in the morning and make us go to the bed of the one who had a birthday, and we'd sing a silly birthday song about birthday cakes making themselves round and fat in honor of the birthday child. It was a remnant bit of affection left over from the time when we were infants, when Father enjoyed playing with us. As we grew older and self-unconscious behavior between us became more self-conscious, signs of affection on the part of Father had petered out so that this remnant bit of birthday custom made us all feel pretty strange.

I wished that I could spend my birthday with Leon. He would buy me some flowers or candy, I was sure, and he would say something nice to me. I was daydreaming about the event, but my mind could not imagine what kinds of words he might say to me. I never had a boyfriend before, and I didn't know if it was right for me to think of Leon as one, but to think of myself as someone's girlfriend made me almost giddy with excitement. As it turned out, his birthday was only four days from mine. "Why don't we celebrate them together," he suggested. "We could do it on the Sunday between our days. You could ride home with me on my motorcycle. I always spend the weekend at home. What do you say?"

"Oh, I'd love to," I sighed. "But Mother probably won't let me."

"You're going to ask, right?"

"I don't know."

He was quiet for a moment, and then he said, "you have to ask her."

"That's easy for you to say. You don't know my Mother. She'll say 'no' if I ask, and then she'll beat me up if I do it anyway."

"I can't believe she would do that."

"Like I said, you don't know my Mother."

"Maybe you should introduce me to your parents. When they see that I'm not a monster...?" and he smiled encouragingly.

I didn't have the heart to tell him that his profession was probably more of a handicap than being a monster. A monster with money would be more readily acceptable, or someone from an old and prestigious local family. A journeyman butcher – and worse - a refugee from the East and the pre-war homeowner of a post-war rubble pile – none of that for Father who prided himself in being a member of the local merchant gentry, who owned a family coat of arms with designated colors of blue and silver. Father never knew that anyone could buy a coat of arms.

"If you don't stand up to your Mother, you'll never be free to do what you want," Leon said gravely. The thought of it scared me almost as much as the tone of his voice. Perhaps he would give up on me if I were never available. I promised to do something about it. I lay awake for hours that night, trying to come up with a non-fatal plan for sharing the day with Leon, but fear of the consequences shot down every image of joy and happiness that my mind could envision. After a lot of mulling and thinking and weighing, and getting no sleep because of it, I decided to simply stop caring about the consequences. After all, what could my parents possibly do to me that they hadn't done before me to Erna and Paula. I remembered some pretty ugly scene when they pulled the "bad" one out of bed and let her have it with fists and even feet. I would be with Leon, come what may. With that happy thought I fell asleep

My plans didn't matter anymore. On the following Wednesday, not seeing Leon right away made me feel anxious. I hoped that he was just late. Minute by minute went by and Leon did not appear. By the time reality set in that he would not show at all, my insides had tied themselves into a heavy, nauseous knot.

The teacher had no information from or about Leon. She paired me up with one of her former students, a member of her emergency fill-in group. He seemed rather aloof, but took much pleasure in showing off his skill and denigrating mine. Mother was pleased with me for coming home early that night.

Housework and looking after the children - Hildi's trouble with math and reading, Hans' profound questions about life and the universe which I could only wonder about but never answer, and the little boys' petty quarrels and spats - provided some diversion from my painful thoughts about Leon.

I was an emotional wreck by the time the next class rolled around. Hope that Leon would come and fear that he would not were an emotional roller coaster ride of the worst sort. But again, Leon did not come. The inner knot seemingly turned to stone. Tears began to well up in my eyes and it took all the will power I had to keep them from overflowing. I made a mental list of all the events that can make a person late, that he forgot, that he was sick, that he had to do something for his Mother, that he was called out of town, that he had a motorcycle accident. When I could no longer pretend that he would yet come, I left. On my way home through the castle grounds I sat down at a linden tree that was graced with a circular bench around its massive trunk. There I sat and cried. For a long time I could not stop crying. When I had no more tears left, I went home. The Protestant church bell rang eleven. I didn't care. Mother's eyes spit fire, her mouth was set hard, but the bright light over the door surely exposed my tear-swollen eyes and smeared face, and perhaps it brought out some feelings of compassion. She said nothing.

My mind tried to come to grips with the loss of Leon, mulling over and over again all the possible scenarios, none of which was any worse than the idea that he simply didn't want to be with me anymore. Finally, I went to Brandt's butchery to ask about Leon. The store was full of women, some of whom could well know me without me knowing them, and I was afraid to ask out loud for fear of the grape vine. Finally, I managed to squeeze through to the end of the counter where I could whisper my question to one of the sales girls behind the counter. She told me that Leon had moved to Munich to work in his brother's butchery. She knew nothing else, and her matter-of-fact response, devoid of any pity or compassion, brought out the tears again.

Without saying good-bye, was all I could think of as I plodded home, wrapped in a shroud of pain and constantly fighting tears. Mother was annoyed with me for taking too long to bring home the groceries. She seemed to be in a bad mood, and her indifference to my pain, of which she knew nothing, made me hurt even more. My tears began to flow again, I didn't try to hide them, but Mother didn't notice.

Hildegard noticed, though, when she came home from school. She had an instinctive way of knowing the right thing to do in a crisis. Without saying a word, she simply wrapped her arms around me, pressed her face against me and just waited till I stopped crying.

"You lost your boyfriend, didn't you," she said when I had composed myself.

"How do you know?" I asked, amazed at her insights.

"I can tell," she simply said, and this child of ten years looked at me with such compassion that I cried again.

"Why can't Mother be more like you," I sighed.

"Her feet hurt too much," she said. "And sometimes her back hurts, too."

On the morning of my birthday Mother said "happy birthday," handed me a chocolate bar, and informed me that it was our turn to wash and wax the stairway the coming weekend. Before I could hide the chocolate in my apron pocket Markus saw it and wanted a share. Of course Matthias had to have some, and I couldn't possibly refuse Hildegard a piece, and finally even Hans, who was never very demanding, ogled my chocolate, of which very little was left for me. Then off to school they went.

Besides the usual Sunday sheet cake for afternoon coffee, Mother told me to bake a layer cake as well. I went shopping for groceries for the weekend, took the big sheet cake to the bakery at the end of the street, where Leon and I had turned about on our dancing nights, made potato soup and sausages for lunch, coffee for Father, then picked up the cake from the bakery and finished cleaning the kitchen. Hildi had already washed the dishes. After the kids had done their homework I gave Markus and Matthias a bath in our tub that was big enough to hold four little kids at once. Around four in the afternoon, Paula and her husband Werner showed up for coffee. Paula had a birthday gift for me. It made me feel so good. It was a set of bath towels. "For your dowry," she said to me in a hushed tone and a smile of encouragement. Werner with the offending eyes wanted to hug me, but I was used to handshakes and backed off.

I had never thought much about what life must have been like for Paula before she was married. It occurred to me now that during the time I was away in Venusbrunn Paula's life must have been pretty much like mine was now. Every minute not spent in Father's business she must have been responsible for doing household chores and looking after the little kids, who were even younger then. But having a full-time housemaid certainly gave her time to go on outings with the Mountain Club of which Werner was a member. And when Erna was still alive, they went together to all sorts of dances, Mardi grass parties, birthday parties, and who knows what else.

"Paula, do me a favor," I said to her when we took the coffee dishes into the kitchen. "Could you talk to Father about letting me work in the office? Or, maybe you should talk to Mother about it. I think she would listen to you now, that you're married. It's funny how you have suddenly become important. She treats you like company."

"That's because Werner is a businessman, with his own shop," Paula said. "Maybe you should find yourself a merchant husband, too."

"And how am I going to do that, stuck in the house in the role of mother and housewife? That's why I want you to talk to Mother about letting me work in the office."

"I'll try. But don't get your hopes up."

"You might point out to her that I'm losing all the skills I learned in boarding school. Surely, she can't want that for me?"

Paula nodded. She knew what I was going through. She had had her share of beatings and verbal abuse, especially when Werner first entered the picture and Paula preferred being at his home instead of ours. It had earned her the 'bitch in heat' euphemism that had since been passed on to me.

I decided not to hang around and watch the agonizing routine of verbal wrestling, which usually lost by us because of Mother's tacit understanding that she was always right. I took the little kids for a walk instead. When we returned, Paula and Werner had left. Walter had come home while I was gone, and he filled me in. It seems that Father had said nothing, Paula had tried her best, even Werner had put in some meaningful comments about my future, but Mother had said that she needed me at home, period. Neither Father nor Mother ever mentioned it again.

I didn't attend the last two classes, and I didn't go to the final ball. Mother never asked the reasons why and I didn't volunteer. This life of mine, which had once been stuck at a dead end that allowed neither vision nor imagination, but which had suddenly experienced color and action, was now stuck at the wall again. And it was worse now because I had seen glimpses of what life could be.

My routine went on as before. Nothing changed except that I became ever more depressed. Hildegard turned twelve in October; both Markus and Matthias had their birthdays in November. The weather was getting cold and my old winter coat was now too short. I tried to convince Mother that I needed a new one.

"There's one in the closet, you can wear that," she said without looking up, occupied with stirring the gravy to prevent lumps.

"You mean Erna's?" Mother didn't answer. I went to try it on. I didn't like its color, didn't like the style, and most certainly didn't like the fact that Erna had once worn it.

"It's too short for me," I told Mother. "I'm taller than Erna." Mother took one quick, unfocused look in my direction and said that it was fine.

Utterly frustrated, I slammed the door as I left the kitchen to hang out in the bathroom, the only room in the house with a key to its lock, the only place where privacy was granted or even possible – until Father needed to get in. I wished Father would interfere on my behalf, I wished Mother was dead, only the realization that I would permanently be tied to my four siblings kept me from giving any power to that wish. As was always the case, I began to feel calmer as I listened to the music from the theater. The movie sound track, that repeated in regular two-hour intervals from eleven o'clock on, could be heard from our playroom window, the kitchen window, but best of all from the bathroom window because it was only a few yards from the projection room door and window. Sometimes, the music was soothing, at other times rousing, but my favorite music rang like echoes of the wide-open American West and became a perfect backdrop and invitation for escape into daydreaming. But inevitably, someone would rattle the door to signal a need to come in.

Later that day, after Mother had gone downstairs and while the children were doing homework, I rummaged through Mother's drawers in the hope of finding some chocolate. It was the only form of retaliation I could come up with, a need to punish her, to inflict injury. Instead of chocolate, though, I found money hidden under a stack of underwear and with it a letter that was addressed to me. It was open.

A gasp of surprise and outrage escaped me when I realized that the letter was from Leon. He had written it right after leaving Hanfurt. He said he was sorry to leave so suddenly and without saying good-bye, that his brother needed a journeyman butcher right away, and that he would have a good chance to work toward becoming a Master butcher there. He was sorry to leave, but he would be back to visit his family. He asked that I write back to let him know if he could visit me, too.

While I was reading, something inside of me went numb. I could see that none of my care and obedience, much less my work, had ever been appreciated by Mother. There would be no more caring on my part. I took letter and money and went to my room. I pulled out from under my bed the small suitcase that I had kept there since graduation from the convent school in Venusbrunn. After throwing out Hildi's doll things I packed a few clothes and toiletries. The children were doing homework when I left. "Fannie?" I vaguely heard Hildi calling after me before the apartment door closed. I walked up the street toward the railroad station not caring if Mother saw me through the large store window. I bought a one-way ticket for Wiesenthal; a train was to leave in twenty minutes. While I was waiting on the platform, pacing up and down, asking, no, screaming inwardly, how could she do that to me! How could she do that to me! How could she do that to me! I was raging with anger and hatred. By the time the train rolled into the station the shock had worn off enough for sensation to return, and my tears began to flow. I hurried into the nearest car, stepped into the nearest empty compartment, flung myself into the window corner and cried. I cried and cried, I could not stop, and it was as though all the suppressed emotions caused by all the harsh words and rejections and beatings of the past were now surfacing to collect their due, and the sheer force of it overwhelmed me.

I must have fallen asleep. Someone shook me by the arm. I looked up. For a moment I had no idea where I was. A conductor asked to see my ticket. Then I remembered. I pulled it out and showed it to him. He looked gravely at me when he said, "your ticket is only good for Wiesenthal."

"Yes, I know," I said. "Are we there yet?"

"We passed Wiesenthal an hour ago," he answered, and my mind shifted into panic mode. Oh my God, I thought. Now what'll I do. I looked to him for answers; after all, he was the adult, and as a railroad employee even a sort of man of the world. Surely he had a magic wand that would make everything come out all right.

"Well, Miss, normally, I would have to ask you to pay for riding this far. But I can see that it was just a mistake. Do you always sleep so soundly?"

"You could carry me away in my sleep and I wouldn't wake up," I whined.

The conductor chuckled, and then said, "you can get off in Augsburg and take a train back to Wiesenthal."

To go to Wiesenthal at this hour of the evening worried me. Would I even have enough money for a ticket. And even if I did have enough money, it could well be in the middle of the night before I got there. I had heard stories about soldiers roaming the streets and molesting girls at night.

When the train rolled into Augsburg's terminal, I reached to take down my small suitcase from the upper compartment. It was gone. A gasp of outrage escaped me. How dare somebody deprived me of the right to clean underwear! I had nothing left but what was in my purse, the handles of which I had slipped over my arm, or it might have been stolen too. I was scared.

The platform was ugly, cold and drafty. I found out very quickly that, just as I had feared, a ticket to Wiesenthal cost more money than I had left. What to do? Where to go? The misery over Mother's underhanded behavior doubled in the light of my present predicament. I looked around, searched for something. Trains steamed in and out of the terminal with hissing airbrakes, conductors whistled, people rushed back and forth. Huge bright lights against the soot-blackened bewildering jumble of pillars and beams and posts, that supported the sooty glass roof, created an image of such unreality that I felt as though trapped in a sinister movie.

I walked this way, then turned and walked that way. I had no idea where I should go and what I should do. But, surely, someone would detect the distress in my face and would offer to help. There were plenty of people all around, each with a goal and a destination, but none of them included me. Their imagined indifference to my plight made me feel terribly isolated and hurt. I couldn't have felt worse if I had been invisible.

In my hurry to run away I had left home in my knee-high stockings. Now, the cold draft blowing up my skirt made my bare thighs feel like ice. When I spied the sign to the Third Class waiting room I went inside quickly. It had a large waiting area with seating, tables, and food services. Quite a few people were passing the time waiting for their next train, some of them eating, reading, or just sitting in a quiet stupor. The warmth felt good; I took off my coat and sat down at a small table and suddenly felt very hungry. At the nearby counter I ordered a sandwich and a glass of milk. Eating did not distract me for very long, and soon I was confronted again with the dilemma of what to do now.

I knew that I could always call home. My parents would definitely send me the money for a return ticket, even if for no other reason than for Mother to get her cheap housemaid back. But that was out of the question, I heard myself thinking in Mother's own words, so often said with shameless indignation as if I had asked to go to the moon. And the only way I had been able to deal with the resultant rage of helplessness and frustration was to go to my room and stick out my tongue in her direction. Pitiful.

What to do. I had no living grandparents but several aunts and uncles, yet I was not close enough to them, did not feel free to call on any of them for help. And I certainly could not call Steffi's parents to bail me out.

People were coming into the waiting room, and others were leaving. The large clock above the door to the platforms struck ten and I was still sitting and thinking. After a while, my butt began to hurt because, as I saw it, my sitz bones had been assembled the wrong way. It had earned me many reprimands for fidgeting from teachers who never bothered to ask the reasons why, but always assumed that I was fidgeting out of boredom and spite.

I looked around for a bench to lie on but they were all occupied. Leaning forward, though, gave my behind some relief. I put my arms on the table, slung my purse around my left arm, laid my head on my arms and hoped to fall asleep quickly and thoroughly.

It was a long night. Every hour or so I woke up to change position. Eventually, a bench became free and served me as a hard bed with nothing but my winter coat to cover the entire length of my tall body. By early morning I couldn't stand it anymore. I went to the restroom, splashed some water on my face, combed my hair, cleaned the moss off my teeth with my finger, and tried not to think about the condition of my underwear. The thought that I might be starting a period had me intensely worried. Then I went back to the waiting room and ordered a doughnut for breakfast. It was a short-lived pleasure that got spoiled by the thought that I should have gotten something cheaper. Then, once again, I was faced with the question of what to do next.

I walked out into the city, walked the streets aimlessly, but this time without any sense of adventure. The sun came out for a little while before it started raining again. When I got too cold, I roamed department stores, bought a banana and French roll for lunch. I went into every church I came by. They were usually empty. Sitting in a pew, in the silence of old architecture reminiscent of my parish church, surrounded by the odor of chrysanthemums and candlelight brought some comfort of spirit. But the churches were too cold to stay long, and they had no toilets. Few stores provided such conveniences. Public restrooms were few and far between and stank to high heaven.

What pained me most was the thought of Hildegard getting slapped around by Mother who was probably in her worst mood ever. Poor Hildi. The boys would be all right because Mother had more respect for the male of the species. She waited hand and foot on Father; she'd sit at the edge of her chair, ready to jump should Paula's husband need something. Even Walter got treated with a certain degree of deference. She did not expect him to do any housework; we girls, on the other hand, had to do housework even when we had housemaids. Even wood and coal for heating and cooking, which could be pretty heavy stuff, we girls had always brought up from the warehouse cellar. Now that Erna und Paula were no longer part of the household, and Hildi was small, Hans often helped me with that chore. Thinking back on how Mother had treated Erna and Paula I suspected that she did not like girls. But if she didn't like girls, how could she like herself? After all, she was a girl too, an old girl, yes, but still a girl. And if she didn't like herself, how could she live with herself? Perhaps that was part of the problem with Mother and why she always seemed so unhappy.

Poor Hildi. She could be so sweet, and yet so obstinate. I feared for her. Then it occurred to me that I could always go back. I could shield her from Mother's impatient outbursts because I sensed that her learning problems had something to do with the way her mind worked, not with stubbornness of which Mother always accused her. But what about me? What about my problems? Who would look out for me? I wouldn't be of legal age until I turned twenty-one. That meant three more years at home with Mother. It was too much to bear.

By late afternoon I went back to the station and prepared for another night on a cold hard bench in the Third Class waiting room. After drudging around in wet streets all day my feet and legs were almost numb with cold. It would not be a good night. The young woman at the counter looked at me with interest. "Weren't you here last night?" she asked.

In fear of being kicked out I said, "why are you asking?"

"I thought you might need some help," she answered less friendly and turned away.

Yeah, sure, she's going to give me money so I can get back to Wiesenthal, I thought in defense against the fact that I had turned her away with nothing more than the tone of my voice. I sat down at one of the tables again, propped my arms on it and dozed off very soon. The day's walking and constant effort to stay warm in the cold and wet November air had made me very tired. Depression over my predicament added its own kind of weariness. Oh, how I longed for a hot bath in our very large and deep bathtub, in which my entire body could be submerged and warmed through and through.

Someone squeezed my arm and I woke up. A middle-age woman looked down at me with a kind smile. "I'm Frau Hartmann from the Railroad Mission," she said. "We look after travelers in need, and it seems to me that you have a need, huh?"

"Oh yes!" it came out of my mouth with a great sigh. Grateful tears rose in my eyes. "I fell asleep in the train and ended up here in Augsburg. That was yesterday. I don't have enough money to leave." I did not reveal where I had come from.

"And you don't know anyone in Augsburg?" she asked.

"No."

"Where is your luggage?" she asked.

"Somebody stole it while I was asleep."

"Oh dear! What about your parents?"

"I can't go back there," I said.

"Why not?" she asked with much compassion in her voice. Tears rose in my eyes at the thought that such tender compassion did exist, yet there had never been any for me. Why did I not want to go back? I couldn't tell her. After all, what could I possibly complain about? Didn't I have a roof over my head? Didn't I get three square meals a day and even more? Didn't my parents call the doctor when I was sick? There was no way she would understand what it was like to have no freedom to be myself, no rights, no privileges but only duties and responsibilities.

"I don't want to talk about it," I said.

"Well, I don't think you should spend another night at the station. Come with me," she said and lead the way out of that nightmarishly unreal terminal. The large clock showed that it was past midnight, but it could have been 5:00 o'clock in the morning for all I knew. I had lost all sense of time. Once outside, she took me by the hand and led me across the street to a nearby low building with a sign above the door that identified it as the Railroad Mission.

She called on someone to bring me something to eat, and after I had eaten with great relish, she showed me the bathrooms, then took me to a women's dormitory. In the dim light from the hallway I could see perhaps twenty simple beds, most of them appeared lumpy, from which I deduced that they were occupied. It reminded me of boarding school in Venusbrunn and made me feel right at home. Frau Hartmann showed me to an empty bed near the door.

"Go to sleep now," she whispered. "We'll talk in the morning. Good night."

Long before daybreak I heard people moving around, whispering, coming and going in and out of the dormitory. I lay awake for a while and watched and listened to the commotion that included a number of dialects that I couldn't quite follow. There were mostly girls and young women, but also a few old women whose heavily lined faces had recorded a great deal of suffering.

From Aunt Elizabeth I had heard stories about what people had endured during World War II and especially after it had ended. Aunt Elizabeth was not an aunt by blood, she was Father's sister's husband's brother's wife's sister, but we liked her very much. Her husband and three of her four boys had died during that war. She had lost her home and all possessions in the Eastern European territorial upheavals, and then even her only surviving son had gotten separated from her during the long trek from the East to the West of Germany. Her wedding ring was all she had been able to save by tying it into a filthy handkerchief that she used to wipe her nose every time Russians or Poles searched her and everyone else on the trek for valuables.

When I began to feel hungry, I got up. A shower, I felt, was rather useless unless I had some clean underwear to put on. I went to the office. Frau Hartmann was not there, but an aid, an older woman told me that she would be coming in around noon. "Breakfast?" she said sternly. "Just follow all the others. And when you're done, come back here to fill out some papers."

"Actually, I was hoping that, maybe, you have some clean underwear I could use. Someone stole my luggage and I've been in the same clothes two days and two nights now," I said.

"Of course. We do have second-hand garments for such emergencies," replied the lady and called for someone. A little woman appeared, short, squat, and with an eye patch over her left eye. Her face was wrinkled like a prune. She wore a bandana around her head and tied it under her small gray hair knot deep on the back of her neck. One could always recognize a refugee from Eastern regions by the bandana. The little woman gave a friendly cackle that exposed yellowed irregular teeth.

"Follow me," she said and limped ahead. "No need to be ashamed. We see all sorts of girls and women here, and they all need something. Now, what is it you need?"

"Some underwear would be nice. I've been in mine for two days now," I whispered.

"Try two weeks," she said as though my two-day relationship with one set of underwear was nothing to be pitied for. "Two weeks," she repeated, "no, two months, without a change of clothes, with babies and children, on a trek through East Prussia in the middle of winter," she said and wiped her eyes with her sleeve. We had reached a small storeroom that was lined with shelves on which stood baskets of all sorts of clothing. "There you go. Take what you need," she said.

I rummaged through the piles and found some panties that would fit. They were not new, and the thought of wearing used panties was not easy to get used to. I also came across some bloomers of the kind that Mother usually gave us for Christmas presents. They were long enough to cover half one's thighs, were made of a thick material that is fleece on the inside and silky knit on the outside, and they were definitely warm. With new appreciation I took them. I also found a blue pullover, some knee socks and even a pair of heavy cotton panty hose and a canvas bag to carry them in. I could have kicked myself when I thought how I had wandered the city all day, cold and numb and hungry, while I could have come here, be warm and fed.

Showers in individual booths provided privacy. Soap, shampoo and clean towels were available, and after washing myself head to toe and thoroughly enjoying the hot water, I got into clean clothes and felt human again.

After breakfast, which consisted of bread, margarine, jam and roasted barley coffee, I went back to the office. Miss Helmer, the lady who had directed me to the dining room, asked me to fill out some forms. I was worried. Being underage, perhaps the Mission would contact my parents. Upon asking about the use of these forms, the woman explained to me that the Mission is funded by federal, state, and private donations, and the staff was required to show how the money was spent. "Don't worry," she said. "We're not going to contact your parents if you don't want us to." I began writing.

When I was finished, Miss Helmer said that Frau Hartmann would conduct my interview and that I should wait for her in the dayroom where I found magazines to read, picture puzzles and other table games. Some girls were also present, and after a while we started talking, and I learned about some very unhappy circumstances compared to which my life was a rose garden. Some of the older girls had lost parents or siblings, got raped or injured in other ways during the war, were pretty much on their own now, and lived at the Mission while trying to find work. Others had run away from an abusive home and needed temporary shelter. One older, fiercely independent woman, who had been traumatized by events of the war, rode the trains in hope of finding her husband and daughter. Her little girl had been separated from her, and the woman had been searching for her ever since. At the Mission, she found a temporary abode and three square meals; in exchange she provided simple services, such as emptying the garbage, sweeping the street in front of the building, and cleaning the restrooms.

Frau Hartmann came and took me to a small room next to the office. "Did you sleep well?" she asked.

"Oh yes, very well, thank you," I replied.

"Now, tell me, what can we do to help you."

"I was on my way to Wiesenthal to visit my girl friend when I fell asleep and missed my stop. That's how I ended up here in Augsburg. I don't have money to buy a ticket to Wiesenthal."

"What about your parents?" She asked, watching me closely. She must have deduced from the expression on my face that not all was well at home, because she continued, "you ran away?" I nodded.

"Do your parents know where you are?"

"They'll think that I went to Wiesenthal."

"Does your girl friend know that you are coming?"

"No, I didn't have a chance to call her. We know each other from boarding school. I've been to her home and her parents know me, and she has been to my house and my parents know her. I know I'll be welcome by her parents."

"And you still want to go there?"

"Yes, sure."

"All right then. Would you like the Mission to pay for a train ticket for Wiesenthal?"

"Oh, that would be great!"

"We do have a policy of re-payment. That means if you should in the future be able to pay back the cost of the ticket we would like you to do that. That way, we can continue to help others. How do you feel about that?"

"Oh, sure. That's only fair. I want very much to work in an office, and if I find such a job, I'll be earning money, and then I can repay you."

"Of course you don't have to pay this particular Mission. If there's one in Wiesenthal, you can pay there, alright?"

"I promise," I said.

"So, let's call up your friend now and let her know you're coming. And I'll call your parents to let them know you're alright."

I squirmed in my seat at the thought of talking to my parents. Frau Hartmann dialed, and pretty soon Steffi herself was on the phone. Frau Hartmann asked to speak to her mother, and then she explained who she was, where she called from, and why she called. From her facial expression I gathered that everything went as I expected. Then she gave me the phone with a smile.

"Hallo?" I said.

"Hallo, Stephanie. You're coming for a visit?"

"Yes, if that's alright with you."

"Certainly. We'll talk when you get here. Just call me from the station so we can come and pick you up."

"Oh, you don't need to do that. I remember where you live, and it's not far from the station, and besides, I don't have any luggage this time. It was stolen."

"That's too bad, dear. Well, come on then. We'll expect you by evening."

I put down the receiver, and Frau Hartmann called someone. A young woman appeared and was told by Frau Hartmann to find out when the next train for Wiesenthal would leave and what the price of a third-class one-way ticket would be. Meanwhile, Frau Hartmann held out her hand for my parents' phone number. "You don't have to talk to them," she said. I just want them to know that you're safe. Of course, you may talk to them, if you want?" I shook my head but gave her the number. She dialed, someone answered, and then Frau Hartmann asked for Herr or Frau Sauerling. Then she explained where I was, where I was going, and that I was safe. There was not much said on the other side, and Frau Hartmann hung up.

"I think it was a girl who answered the phone," she said.

"That was Hildegard. How did my Mother sound? I mean, did she sound sad, or upset or anything?"

"No, she sounded quite ordinary; a little harsh and short, perhaps, but polite."

"Did she say that I should come back?"

"No. And I think she had already figured out that you went to visit your girl friend."

"That's what I thought."

Frau Hartmann continued talking, but her words drowned in my thoughts about Mother. Supposedly, she couldn't manage without me but now she did just fine. To my surprise, I felt rejected and hurt. For well over a year Mother had me working long days. I had no vacations, no days off, not even pay that could have afforded me some pretty clothes. And now, all of a sudden, she didn't need me. Well, that suited me just fine. I would not feel guilty anymore.

The young woman came back and reported that a train would leave in forty-five minutes. "That gives you time for lunch," said Frau Hartmann. "Then come back to the office and we'll have the ticket for you." I felt elated at the though of being able to see Steffi that very day and putting this nightmare behind me. I thanked Frau Hartmann and went to the dining room.

When it was time to leave, the young woman accompanied me as far as the turnstile, beyond which only ticketed passengers were allowed. She handed me the ticket, we shook hands, and said good-bye. I headed for the platform on which my train would leave. As I waited for the train to roll in, I saw, beyond two sets of tracks on the next platform, a figure of a man with blond hair. It was short, curly, and stood straight up at the forehead. When the man turned to face my platform I saw that it was Leon. At the same instant, Leon saw me and his eyes grew wide with surprise. "Stephanie?" he shouted across the tracks.

"Leon?" I shouted back. A train pulled in on his platform, huffing and puffing and airbrakes hissing. If he said anything more, I could not hear it. I hurried back to where the tracks terminated, hoping he would do likewise, and sure enough, Leon came running around the engine. Our eyes met and we grinned from ear to ear.

"Why didn't you write?" he asked.

"I thought you live in Munich now" I said at the same instant.

"I do," he replied. "I just came for the weekend to visit one of my brothers. But why didn't you write? Didn't you get my letter?"

"It's a long story," I said and suddenly felt a flush of exhilarating joy come over me. Everything about Leon - his smile of utter contentment, his affectionate demeanor with which he held my hand, his eyes that kept holding mine, everything about him told me that he loved me. A remarkable sense of unshakable certainty that we belonged together took hold of me. I kissed him on the cheek and said, "my train is coming in and yours is probably leaving any minute. I have your address and I'll write to you, for sure – I'll explain everything."

A quick hug from Leon and he hurried back to his platform while I ran to meet my train to Wiesenthal that came to a screeching halt. I climbed aboard, rolled down the window and looked for Leon. He did the same thing, and we stood face to face, yet in two different trains on two different platforms, smiling at one another.

"What were you doing in Augsburg?" he shouted to me.

"I'm here by mistake," I shouted back. "But I'll tell you all about it. Right away. Tomorrow. As soon as I get to Wiesenthal." Somewhere a conductor blew a shrill whistle, doors slammed shut, last shouts of good-byes mingled with the chugging of the train as it began to pull backward out of the station. Leon shouted one last "write to me!" and I waved as long as I could see him.

By the time I arrived in Wiesenthal with my head full of thoughts and plans, regrets and hopes, it had grown dreary gray and rainy. Knowing that body and soul would soon be comfortable in a warm and friendly place, though, I didn't mind getting wet. Without luggage, I made it quickly to Steffi's house and rang the bell. And just like the first time I came to visit, a window on the second floor was flung open and Steffi looked down to see who it was. Then her head disappeared and the window slammed shut. Then a pair of leather shoes came thudding down a staircase and ran across a stone floor. The door was yanked open, and out flew Steffi.

"Stef!" she shouted and slung her arms around my neck. I was not used to such effusive shows of affection and it made me feel a bit weird. But I hugged her back, and we laughed and bobbed about like a clump of symbiotic nuts.

"You're drenched," she remarked, stepping back and clasping her chest where she was beginning to feel what my soaking wet overcoat had imparted to her blouse.

"Well, we could go upstairs and wring each other out," I suggested

"Good grief! Come on in, you silly goose," she said and laughed.

She led the way to the upper floor and took me inside her warm, cozy apartment that was filled with an aura of nest warmth that I had never experienced at home. I could have cried. But I figured that it made more sense to enjoy what I had right now instead of mourning what had never been mine.

After I had hung up my wet coat on a hook in the hallway and taken off my wet shoes, I followed her to her room. She had changed a lot from that scrawny little thing I first knew in Venusbrunn four years ago. Scrawny and nervous she had been, with thin black hair hanging around her face that was usually turned down as though she feared getting hit over the head by someone. Eventually, for some reason I never knew, she had confided in me. That's how I learned that Steffi is psychic, that she could see and hear all sorts of beings that no one else could see or hear. It became a real burden for her, because she could never talk about her experiences. I wondered why. Eventually it became clear to me that when no one talks about something, gnomes and fairies for instance, then Steffi, who could see and hear them, would conclude that the subject is taboo, or that something is wrong or weird with her. How sad!

It was even worse when she had visions of bad things happening to someone, and she felt obliged to help but couldn't. Such burdens she had to deal with all by her little lonesome self. She's not thriving, her Doctor used to say to her parents. But he had no idea why.

"What on earth happened?" Steffi asked straight out, interrupting my train of thoughts.

"In Augsburg?"

"Well, that too. But what happened with your Mother that you ran away?"

"You know what she did to me? I wrote you about Leon, and that he left without saying good bye to me, right?" Steffi nodded. "Well, he wrote to me from Munich, but my Mother never gave me the letter. She actually opened it and read it."

"Oh, that's so mean! How could she do that! How did you find out?"

"I rummaged through her things, just day before yesterday. That's when I found the letter. I found some money, too. So I took it and just left. Didn't tell anybody that I was going, or where. Just took off."

"I'm so sorry for you," Steffi said and gave me a hug.

"Don't be," I said. "That trip to Augsburg made up for it. Guess what I found there."

"I have no idea," Steffi said with a big grin, fidgeting in anticipation of something delicious.

"I found Leon."

"Wow, what luck!" Steffi yelled with gleeful sympathy.

"I think he really likes me. His face lit up like a Christmas tree when he saw me. And I thought he didn't care about me when I didn't hear from him."

"It must have been awful," Steffi said.

"And nobody to confide in. But you know what that's like. Funny thing, though, my little sister Hildi is really something. She always knows what's going on with me."

"She can probably see your aura."

"I'm beginning to think so. I'll have to find out. But listen, I need to write to Leon right away. You have writing paper, don't you?"

"It's right there in my desk drawer. Just help yourself."

"And my suitcase got stolen on the train. Just think, I'm asleep in my corner on the train and someone sneaks up to me, makes sure I'm sleeping, and then takes my suitcase and runs. It's so disgusting! Now I only have a few things that I got at the Mission."

"You can borrow from me," she said, looking my beanpole size up and down with a grin. "I think I caught up with you; I've grown some since last year summer, when I came to Hanfurt."

"And you filled out a bit, too; you even have boobs now. And your hair seems thicker. I like your short hair cut. You have just enough natural curl to make it look real cute."

"When are you going to get yours cut?"

"Oh, I'm so tired of that bun. I get really bad headaches sometimes. As soon as I have money, that's when I'm going to have it cut. And I won't be asking anybody's permission either." We laughed. We were sitting on her bed and talked and talked till it was time for Steffi to get things ready for supper.

"I bought all your favorites," she said. "Salami, and Edam cheese, and the bread you like so much." I went to help her. While she made tea in the kitchen, I set the table for a cold supper. Steffi's mother came in a few minutes later. She was hardly taller than I and still slender, had short blond stylishly curled hair, and she wore lipstick and even nailpolish. I loved the sight of glossy red nailpolish on well-manicured fingers. I would have that too, some day.

"Stephanie! I'm glad to see you made it. How are you, Dear?" We shook hands, the way my family was used to doing. Her handshake had a different feel, though. She looked at me, looked me in the face with a glad and pleasant expression. It was like a hug by way of a handshake.

"I'm fine, now. Thanks a lot for letting me come here."

"Any time, Stephanie. We made up a bed for you in Steffi's room. But I expect you already know that. We'll talk some more later," she said, seeing that Steffi's father was now coming in.

"Hi Daddy!" Steffi said and went to kiss him.

Herr Rhein put his arm around her shoulder. "How's my girl?" he asked. "How did the English test go?"

"I think I did alright. Won't know for sure till day after tomorrow, though."

"You're a smart girl. You did okay I know it."

He didn't look like a father, I thought, at least not like my Father who was pushing sixty. Herr Rhein looked young and trim, and his clothes were stylish. He still had a full head of blond hair, and his upper lip cradled a mustache that had a reddish tint. Quite dashing, really. He greeted me with a handshake, and a sly grin played around his mouth as he glanced to his wife who smiled back, just as though they knew a secret and enjoyed knowing it.

Later that evening, dressed for the night in one of Steffi's flannel nightgowns that was too short for me and a little tight around the chest, we perched on the edge of our beds, with knees pulled up under our nightshirts, and my feet trying but failing to find equal shelter therein. We talked about Leon again.

"Say, Steffi, do you have a boyfriend?"

"No, not really. There is a guy who takes music lessons from the same teacher as me. He's kind of cute, I think. He looks at me, and he seems interested, but we never really have a chance because he leaves when I get there. But listen, it's getting late, and I have to go to school tomorrow. Better get to bed now. By the way, how long do you want to stay?"

"Forever," it came out of me as though my mouth were an independent entity unconnected to brain. "Well, not really."

"Hey, it's okay with me. But, of course, we'll have to talk to my parents about it. Maybe they can come up with a good idea for you. Good night, Stef," she said and lay back.

I lay down, pulled the featherbed over me; it, too, was a little short for me, but pulling up my knees into the fetal position did the trick. I lay awake a long time that night, happy to be with people who cared about me, relieved to have escaped the nightmare of being homeless, giddy with joy to have found Leon again - my boyfriend. I dared to think that word, taste it, and dream it.

After we had breakfast the next morning and Steffi had left for school and her Dad for his shop on the street level of their house, Frau Rhein took me to the living room where I told her all that had happened. I figured that finding Leon's letter must have caused a short circuit in my brain, and that had sent me running to the only friend I had. Frau Rhein was a good listener, and it made it easy for me to spill it all, about my life as foster mother and homemaker, that I had no hope of ever doing anything else, and about Leon, whom I had found again at the station in Augsburg. At the mention of Leon, she chuckled. Then she explained that Steffi's father had predicted that a boy was involved in my troubles. Finally, she asked, "well, Stephanie, what do you want to do?"

"I don't really know. My parents never asked me, and I never really thought about it. But I definitely don't want to be stuck in the house anymore."

"Do you want to work in an office?"

"Yes! I would like that a lot better. I would have worked in my Dad's office, but Mother wouldn't let me."

"Do you think it would do any good for me to talk to your parents about letting you work in the office?"

"I don't think so. But you can try. But even if I worked in the office, I'd still end up looking after the kids and doing housework during all the other hours. It wouldn't be so bad if I could get a day off now and then, or even a vacation. And there's no pay either because Father takes it, and supposedly saves it."

Oh, if you could only know what it's like to be standing in the midst of a group of girls, I thought, on the occasion of one of those many pilgrimages that we had to endure. There was the annual fire pilgrimage that was promised by ancestors whose wooden houses caught fire and with it half the town. Then came the annual plague pilgrimage that was promised to God if he ended that dreadful pestilence. And there were pilgrimages to this Saint and that, on this hill and that, to this church and that. But the biggest and grandest of them all, the annual religious procession through town on Corpus Christy Day in early summer, when even houses, streets and squares were decked out in great quantities of the most beautiful and colorful greens and flowers – that was the most painful of all. We girls from our parish would be in a group, as all others - male, female, young, old, religious orders, secular organizations - were grouped together. Daughters of simple workers, self-assured and confident, were dressed in pretty new clothes while I, daughter of the local merchant gentry, felt inhibited and dreadfully inadequate in my single pair of stockings that might develop a run; afraid that my sister's hand-me-down dress was too conspicuous; and that my other sister's winter coat wouldn't look too shabby amid the bright and glorious colors and new fashions of that summer day.

"I should call your Mother and tell her that you are here," she suggested.

"Actually, Frau Hartmann from the Railroad Mission talked with her and told her that I was coming here."

"Still, I will let her know that you made it alright. So, now we need to find you a job. You could go to the employment office and see what's available. You want to do that?"

"Yes, of course!"

"All right. That's what we'll do. I need to go down to the shop now, and after you've written that letter you promised," and she smiled as if she remembered a similar joy from her own youth, "come downstairs and we'll get started."

"And, of course, I'll help around the house. But, please tell me what you want me to do, and how. Even though I'm an expert housekeeper," I couldn't help grinning and feeling a bit proud, too, "you probably have your own way of doing things, right?" Frau Rhein smiled and nodded, then she went out.

Steffi had plenty of writing paper in her desk. I sat down and began writing, but it wasn't easy to come up with the perfect address. Oh, I knew that I wanted to call him Love, or Sweetheart, or simply Dear Leon, but he would be reading it from a piece of paper that offered no tonal inflexion, and therein lay the difficulty. There was nothing to do but write and hope for the best. Dear Leon…

A few days later, on the first Saturday in December, Steffi and I were doing housework when the doorbell rang. Steffi opened the window to see who was there. Then she turned to me with an impish grin and said, "just a stranger; I think I'll send him away." But her smile gave it away.

"Don't you dare!" I yelled and ran to the window. And there he was, Leon, looking up to the window, with that same curly blond hair that stood straight up at the forehead as though it had a mandate to never flatten out. I grinned, he grinned. "I'll be right down," I said.

"I will open the door," Steffi said with dignified and heavy emphasis on the 'I will', grinning, moving slowly ahead of me, spreading both arms to keep me from running past her. I pushed and shoved to get her out of the way, she pushed and shoved back to keep me behind her. We laughed, we yelled, and finally I ducked under her spread arms and ran downstairs. I fairly ripped open the door. Then I stood still to take in the whole picture that was Leon, not just his hair, not just his eyes, but all the memories and words and touches that were embodied in this dear man.

"I'm sorry to show up unannounced," he said as he entered. "But I didn't know if I could get off today, and I didn't want to promise something I couldn't keep." He smiled bashfully as he said it, and his eyes shone and looked deep into mine and roused exquisite butterflies inside me. He shut the door and then pulled me close and hugged me warmly and didn't stop holding me until I had enough.

Then I took Leon by the hand and led him upstairs where Steffi was waiting discreetly behind the door. I introduced them to each other. Steffi's parents were busy in the shop. Steffi offered to do the shopping which I would have done otherwise, so that Leon and I could spend time together. When Frau Rhein came upstairs for lunch, I introduced Leon to her. She seemed pleased; Leon made a good impression on her. To her question where and how long he would stay, Leon explained that he had come by train and would go back Sunday afternoon. He would spend the night in the local youth hostel. During lunch, Steffi's parents had a lot of questions for Leon, about his job, his brother's butcher shop, and his family's escape from the East.

After Herr and Frau Rhein had gone down to the store again, Leon and I went for a walk. He offered me his arm, I put mine in his, and the sun came out to add sparkle to this wonderful day.

"You did get my letter, didn't you?" I asked him.

"Yes, I did. But I'm not much of a letter writer. Talking is better, isn't it?"

"Right," I said. I gloated inwardly about walking arm-in-arm with my boyfriend for all the world to see, no clock to watch, no defensive lie to invent, and no angry Mother waiting for me. Later on we stopped at a little Café for coffee and pastry. It was then that I mentioned to Leon that I had neither money nor clothes.

"You should go home and get your things," he said.

"And face Mother? No way! By the way, what do you think about what she did to me?"

46

"I'm beginning to understand why you feel the way you do about her. But it really doesn't change anything. She's your Mother, and you still need to face her. And how about your little sister and brothers. You left them without a word."

"Yeah, I know," I said with a sigh.

"So, when are you going to do it?"

"Do what?"

"Face her."

"Never!"

"Do you want your parents to treat you like an adult?" I nodded. "Then you have to act like an adult. You need to go home and square things with everybody in your family."

"I know, I know. I kept thinking about it since the time you told me I should assert myself with my mother. I was actually going to do that. Remember, we wanted to celebrate our birthdays together? I had decided to simply go with you and not worry about anything else. But then you were gone. It was awful."

Leon took my hand and kissed it gently. "I'm so sorry," he said. Then he began to tell me about Munich, what a grand old city it was, and how sure he was that I would like it there.

Meanwhile, it began to grow dark. The following Sunday would be the first Sunday of Advent, and people had set up Christmas market in the town square. We walked the aisles of booths, sniffed the wonderful aroma of Christmas goodies, and enjoyed the lights and the crowds. We came to a booth that sold ginger bread in all sorts of shapes and sizes. Some looked like hearts and had words of frosting written on them. They were wrapped in plastic and came with a string to hang around one's neck. Leon bought one for me that read, "For my Sweetheart." I knew those hearts from souvenir booths and felt silly for wearing one, but Leon said, "Just something good to eat – but I mean what it says." He hung the heart around my neck and I was glad to accept and wear it.

Later that evening, after Leon had gone to the youth hostel, I repeated to Steffi what Leon had advised me to do. "He's right," she said. "Besides, I can't understand why you are so timid. In Venusbrunn I was the timid one, and you kept telling me what to do, when to do, and how to do." We laughed at the memory of these days. "But here you are, today, three years older, and you can't face your mother. You faced Mother Superior, didn't you?"

"Yeah, but she was human. You just don't know my mother!" I nearly yelled it to keep that annoying little inner voice from reminding me what I had long suspected - that it was just an excuse.

"You want to get on with your life, don't you? You want to find a job, earn some money, go on a vacation, buy yourself some pretty clothes, right?" said Steffi before we fell asleep. "Well, go to your Father and ask for the money he saved for you. Then you pay back your mother the money you took from her to finance your odyssey to Wiesenthal. Then you tell her so by the way that you won't be coming back. Then you make things right with your little sister and brothers, and you come back here, free and clear. See?"

"I'll think about it," I agreed, but my mind wandered to Leon, snuggled up to him, kissed him, pressed close to him, felt his arms around me so warm, so loving.

Coming back from the station where I had seen Leon off, my mind wrapped itself around the question of what to do next. Christmas was coming. I should be at home then; there was just no other place to be at such a time. Hildi and the little boys were probably waiting for my return like puppies that knew nothing of finality. And I didn't want to miss singing with the choir during midnight mass, up on the gallery, that special place reserved for the musical embellishers of churchly rituals. From high up there one had a grand view of the altar with its rich decorations of flowers and candles that create such a striking contrast to the poignantly austere over-life-size crucifix above. I was baptized in that church and had gone to first Holy Communion there. I had gone to confessions there whenever my guilty conscience yearned for absolution, which, in the religious climate of the time, was almost every Saturday. And there, any day of the week and any time of the day, I had spent many an hour sitting. Just sitting, while the inner storm, brought on by unrequited needs and wants that had grown too burdensome, had worked itself out.

It wouldn't feel right to be at Steffi's house at such an intimate celebration as Christmas. Her parents would surely feel the same way. And I certainly couldn't spend Christmas in Munich with strangers, even though Leon would be there, and even though he had said I could come. His brother could put me up in a spare room, and work would not be hard to find, he had said.

And there was the walk to the cemetery on the afternoon of Christmas Eve to visit the silent, agreeable members of the family that I had never known. It was the somber prelude to the giddy fun of opening presents. I wouldn't miss it for anything. Arm-in-arm, in a steady, rhythmic gait of almost musical quality, three or four of us older children would walk through streets that were deserted by pedestrians and most cars. Stores would close at noon. Young and old would be at home preparing for the holiday.

A fine mist would envelop houses, streets, and us in a thin shroud of mystery that fired the imagination with tingling anticipation. Like the rest of the city, the cemetery would lay silent and utterly deserted. Chrysanthemums, the last remnants of a glorious fall, would grace the base of the gravestone that dominates the family plot. On the stone were engraved the names of Father's parents, his brother Ernst who had died at age fifteen, and Father's handsome brother John who was killed during World War I and lay buried somewhere in France. Father's maiden aunt rested nearby, and in the children's section lay his baby brother and sister.

On All Saints Day, November 1, Mother always set up the three-legged grave lantern in the middle of the large family plot. Then on Christmas Eve, Mother would replace the burned down candle with a new one and would light it with a match, which was always a challenge on a wet, windy day. She would pick dead leaves off the spruce branches that covered the bare soil, and talk about replanting with begonias in the spring. We would say prayers for the strangers we had never known, yet carried within us. That's when Father would turn nostalgic.

The mist would run off trees and shrubs in steady droplets and soak the ground. The damp cold would creep through our shoe soles and rise into our stocking-clad legs and make us anxious to go home. It would get darker on our way back, and colder. Silhouettes of town houses along the streets would stand introspective, silent and dark in the eerie stillness of the lead gray twilight. Through gaps in drawn window curtains we would glimpse festive white candle lights on Christmas trees of highly intimate celebrations.

Christmas Eve was Mother's happy day. On return from the cemetery, she would find a friendly couple waiting for her in the livingroom. While she would enjoy this rare visit, we children would dress in our best clothes and then wait in the playroom till company would leave. Mother would look in on us from time to time to promise that the wait was almost over. She had company so rarely, and the smile on her face would be so blissful that we wouldn't dare complain. And so, we would wait.

With company gone, Mother and Father would do some last minute flitting about in and out of the formal dining room and through it to the piano room where the nativity would be set up. Opposite the nativity stood the glossy black piano that Father had once rescued from the rubble pile of a neighbor's bombed house. Between nativity and piano would be the Christmas tree, a seven foot spruce, emaciated looking in its natural state with branches far apart, but with ornaments hung and fine heavy tinsel reflecting thousand fold the flames of carefully placed white candles, the tree would be a glorious sight to behold.

The dining room and the piano room would be locked until Christmas Eve. When it was time, Mother would come for us with her blissful smile. She and Father would lead us to the piano room to sing Christmas carols, accompanied by one or the other of us older children on the piano, and recite poetry by the nativity. We would ogle the slightly open door that led to the dining room, in hopes of getting a glimpse of the presents that we knew were spread out on table, chairs, and sideboard, for each one of us our own little pile. We wouldn't know which pile belonged to whom until Mother, with her blissful smile, would take us by the hand and lead us to it.

Father would become frisky then. He would sing the song about the Christmas tree with many lights, but he would change the lyrics and would sing about a prune that his dumb brother had hung on the tree. We would know, of course, that he sang about the brother with whom Father managed the family business but could never get along. The words would rhyme so well they would make us laugh, and Mother would scold with mock indignation, "Husband! Stop that!" - Yes, I had to go home for Christmas.

"So you're going, huh?" Steffi said later that night, like a statement of fact that needed verification, or justification. She took her violin from its case and began tuning it.

"Yeah, I have to."

"It's a shame, really. I've gotten used to having you around - like a sister."

"Like a housekeeper, you mean," I teased.

"That too," she said and laughed. Then, more serious and with emphasis, "but only because it gave me more time to practice." She said it with a most dignified expression that, unfortunately, crumbled into undignified giggles. "And you can always come back," she added, and we both laughed at the implication.

To make matters more complicated, Frau Rhein told me the next day that their office help would be leaving by the end of the year. Would I be interested in taking over? I could spend my time between now and then in the office, learning how things were done. I would be paid some money, and it would be more than enough for a train ticket home on Christmas – and surely, I would want to be home for Christmas - or even a two-way ticket, if need be. Overjoyed, I accepted immediately.

"What luck that your office help is leaving," I said to Steffi later. "Your parents are really great for offering me that job. Actually, they are great any which way you look at them. I wish they were mine."

"Sorry, Stef. But, hey! Look at it this way - if your Mother doesn't agree to a few changes you can always come back here. Actually, you can now bribe her into giving you some freedom."

"That's right," I yelled, just now realizing that some level of power was finally mine. "But do I really want to live at home?"

"What about Hildi and your brothers?" said Steffi.

"You're right." And after a lengthy pause I said, "it's settled; I'm going home for Christmas. Don't know if I'll stay, but I can figure that out later. You know something? I just made a decision. Totally on my own. I think I'm emancipated. Wow!"

"Yes, you emancipated silly goose," said Steffi and tapped me on the head with her violin bow. She could not possibly understand the joy in such a simple thing as making one's own decision. Steffi had taken it for granted. Her parents had never controlled, only guided her. And the funny thing was, she had always made the right decision.

Two days before Christmas, on a rainy Wednesday afternoon, I arrived in Hanfurt amid the crowded noise of Christmas shoppers, traffic jams, and the increased glare of neon lights. I figured the kids would be at home, presumably under the supervision of Hans who was next in line of authority, but more likely a new housemaid. Mother would be in the store. A young woman whom I didn't know answered the door.

"I'm Stephanie Sauerling," I said. "I live here." It startled me to hear me saying that I "live" here. The young woman, the owner of a heavy-set body, colorless hair and a steady frown, stepped aside to let me in. Suddenly, a door flung open and Hildi came running into the hallway and the boys after her. She threw herself at me and yelled, "oh Fannie, I knew it was you. I just knew it."

"How?" I asked, greatly relieved by this happily spontaneous outpouring of welcome, the form of which, and how it might be accomplished, I had dreaded since leaving Wiesenthal.

"I don't know," Hildi said, and a slight shadow spread over her face. "I missed you so much. Why did you go away, where were you, why didn't you write?" She hugged me again, and I held her with one arm while I grabbed the little boys with my other arm.

"Why did you go away?" Markus wanted to know.

"Why didn't you say good-bye?" Matthias whined.

"Hey, Sis! I'm glad you're back. I'm tired of looking after these little tyrants," Hans said and tickled the little boys until they squealed and ran away.

"Where did you go? What did you do? Oh, I know: you missed Mother; you just can't live without her," Hans teased.

"Yeah, that's it, for sure," I replied with a laugh. "Well, I'll tell you everything, but first I have to go see Father. He's downstairs, right?"

"Where he always is," remarked Hildi.

Father was sitting at his desk when I came in without knocking. He looked up to see who it was. His face lit up for a moment, but then it took on a sour grimace. "You caused your Mother a lot of trouble," he said but did not get up. I hadn't known what to expect from him and immediately felt myself slipping into the morass of timidity. But I sensed that this was a crucial moment, and that if I didn't handle this moment the right way, I could very well lose out for all time. It gave me strength of will.

Calmly and firmly I said to him, "do you know what Mother did to me? Would you like to know?" Father looked puzzled. It had never occurred to him that a mother-daughter relationship could be a two-way street.

"What did she do?" he asked without any sign of real interest.

"Didn't you ever wonder why I didn't finish dancing school? My partner, Leon, had to leave town suddenly and he wrote to me right afterward. Mother not only opened the letter and read it, she never gave it to me at all. But I found it, and that's when I left."

Father shrugged. I could see that he didn't consider this violation of my privacy important enough to leave Mother in the lurch by running away. But before he had a chance to deflate the profoundness of my justifiable rebellion, I went on to tell him that I would be willing to work in the office but not as house maid; that I expected the rights every employee is entitled to, such as pay and vacations; and, most important, that I wanted the money he had withheld from me for working as a house maid since coming back from Venusbrunn.

"I put that money in your account to save for later," he objected.

"I need it now," I said. "I need to pay Mother back for what I took from her. And I need to pay the Railroad Mission for the ticket to Wiesenthal that they bought for me. And besides, I could use some decent clothes. And you should know that I can go back to Wiesenthal, because I have an office job waiting there for me. You can discuss it with Mother." With that I turned and left his office. I was shaking. My heart was beating so hard I could hear it in my ears. Out in the stairwell, I had to stop for a moment to savor the tremendous sensation of pride and satisfaction that was welling up in me. I had dictated my wishes to my parent. Careful, whispered the inner voice.

Hans and Hildegard were all ears when I explained to them what had happened. They knew that before long they could well be in similar positions as I was faced with right now. The little boys went on playing; they were just happy that I was back. Then I noticed something on Hildi's cheek. "Are those welts?" I asked.

Hildi nodded. "Mom hit me because I had trouble with some of the words from a story she wanted me to read. I really tried, but I just couldn't."

"She's right. I was there," said Hans who never had trouble learning anything.

"What kind of story was it?"

"A hard one for sure," said Hans. "From Blunk's Fairytales."

I knew that book of regional tales and legend with the most wonderful watercolor illustrations but archaic language and archaic type. Even I had hardly done more than look at the pictures

"Well, don't you worry," I said, playing with Hildegard's braids that had obviously been worked by a person of little experience. "I'm here now." With that, alarm bells went off in my head. Was that a promise to stay?

Hans had gone back to reading his book, the little boys were playing with an old hand-me-down erector set that had lost many of its parts. They boys didn't seem to notice or care. Hildegard wanted me to read to her, which I did. After a time the door opened and Mother came in. She stopped dead in her tracks for a moment when her eyes caught sight of me. A barely perceptible tightness spread across her mouth while she looked around from one to the other. Stalling for time, I figured. My insides went on alarm, the morass of timidity beckoned, but I forced myself to remain calm. Mother left the room without saying a word.

Hildi searched my face with her eyes; I smiled, satisfied at having successfully passed the second trial. I knew that more were to follow. I learned from Ilse how long ago she had been hired, how many hours she was expected to work, and what her duties were. She occupied the attic room, as many of her predecessors had done. Once per month she was free to go home from Saturday afternoon through Sunday evening. I spent the evening with the children. At bedtime, we gathered around the advent wreath, on which Hans had lit all four red candles, to say prayers. Then off to bed they went.

Hildi was happy to have me share her room again. She wrapped her arms around my neck and clung to me longer than she had usually done. Suddenly, she said, "you're happy now; I think you found your boyfriend again, didn't you." I had wanted to ask her if she could see auras, yet I didn't want to influence her in any way by naming that which I wanted to know.

"Hildi, how on earth do you know these things?" I asked.

"Oh, I don't know. Maybe it's the pretty colors around your body that makes me know."

"Pretty color around my body?"

"Yeah, You know. Pinks and blues and yellows. Some people have real ugly colors; they scare me. But yours are pretty, and they make me know that you're happy." While she snuggled into her featherbed, she asked with a touch of sadness in her voice, "I wonder what Christmas will be like this year, without Erna and Paula."

"Oh, it'll be just fine, you'll see. Getting presents is always fun, isn't it." Hildi smiled.

"I remember one year, about three years ago, when we had a terrible storm. It rained buckets and the wind howled like crazy; it actually blew down one of the chimneys. We didn't know that, of course, until old Mrs. Moser from the fourth floor came down, in the middle of the night, in her nightgown, and told us that she had a puddle of water in her bed." Hildi giggled with delight. "Well, Erna, Paula and I had to go up that narrow dingy dark stairway to the attic under the roof, go out across that little metal bridge to the flat warehouse roof, and then bring in some of the metal tubs that were stored there in our old playhouse that nobody plays in anymore. We put them under the drips and that took care of it for the night."

"Didn't you get wet?" Hildi asked.

"Of course we got wet! Soaking wet in pajamas and robes. But it was kind of exciting – different, you know. Next morning, Father called Herr Stulier, who lives just a few blocks away, and had him put up barricades on the sidewalk until the rubble from the chimney could be removed. Another year, Hans got real sick. He turned white as a sheet and had terrible headaches. Mother called the doctor. I don't know what the trouble was. One other year it was Markus. He had a bad ear infection. Another year, and that was the worst, it was Mathias who was just one year old when he came down with polio. That was a bad thing. You don't remember that, do you?"

Hildi shook her head. It didn't actually surprise me, because I had not known it myself until years later. It happened while I was still at Venusbrunn. The other kids had to stay quarantined at home. Too many kids "hanging out in a pile," as Mother was used to saying. It made her nervous, I guess, so Mother never told me about the polio and sent me back to Venusbrunn. It was four years later that I found out quite by chance from an outsider.

Hildi had grown sleepy. I kissed her, said good night and went to watch a little television. Father seemed pleased to see me, but neither said anything to me. The program was a satire with Heinz Ruehmann, a great actor, in the lead role. Mother laughed as I have seldom seen her laugh. A little while into the play, she asked me to get some more beer from the cellar, and it was quite as though nothing had ever changed. It made me rather uneasy, for I feared that consequences for my running away were still in store for me. When the play and the late news were over and the television turned off, there was a quiet pause, into which I said out loud, "Mother, Dad, what do you want me to do tomorrow?"

Mother said, "Henkel is going to bring the Christmas tree tomorrow. You could get the decorations from the attic and decorate it. We'll put up the tree in the big room and keep it locked until Christmas Eve. And then you can do the shopping."

"But, what about work, I mean, a job in the office?"

"After Christmas," Father said. "In the meantime you can help your Mother the rest of this week and next while the children are home from school."

"And will I get paid what other people get?"

"We'll talk about that later. Your Mother wants to dress my leg now," Father said and got up from his chair. I had watched the dressing of his leg once; it had a large blue-black circular area on the outside of the calf that, we had been told, was the result of a gunshot wound he had received in WWI. If we had ever talked about personal matters, I would have learned much earlier that it doesn't take forty years to heal a gunshot wound.

The days until Christmas passed quickly and happily. Ilse did the housework, and I could spend all my time with the kids. While Hans watched the little boys between pages of his ever-present book, I did some of the grocery shopping and took Hildi with me. To go into a small specialty shop with its polite salespeople was always a pleasure. But shopping the large stores was a nightmare for me. Having entered in a heavy winter coat meant for outdoors, the heat that was created by the crowd that moved thick and slow like porridge through the narrow isles of the store, became unbearable. Being quick and not having much patience, I used my elbows to get ahead, dragging Hildi behind and in constant fear of losing my grip on her.

The tree was delivered during late morning, while the boys were in the living room and the door to the hallway was shut. Henkel, an employee from the store, was able to take the seven-foot spruce, already fastened in its stand, to the big room. Then Ilse locked the door and removed the key. That night, after the kids were in bed, I went to the attic and brought down the decorations. Putting up the ornaments put me in a happy mood. Mother popped her head through the door to see how it was coming along. Then I clipped on the candleholders, placed the white tree candles, and hung the tinsel.

Christmas fell on Friday that year, followed by the second Christmas holiday on Saturday. Ilse joined her family for Christmas and would not return until Sunday evening. Just as Hildi had feared, things were not as they used to be on Christmas Eve without Erna and Paula. We did not go to the cemetery, the children got antsy and could not concentrate on anything useful, Walter came and went as if our household had nothing to offer him except food, bed, and laundry services. He loved soccer, Father cared about politics. Walter had newfangled ideas about the pros and cons of a German army, conscientious objecting and domestic self-reliance. Father, a WWI veteran under Kaiser Wilhelm II, could not relate. It produced much tension during dinnertime and was only mitigated when it became time to visit the nativity, sing Christmas carols and open presents. Father did sing about the plum that his dumb brother had hung on the tree, we laughed, and Mother scolded in mock indignation, "husband, stop that!"

I looked forward to singing the midnight mass with the choir up on the gallery. Then, at the end of mass, all the lights would go out except for the multitude of candles at the altar and two large evergreen trees, to the right and left of it. Then, the organ would play Silent Night, people would join in, and tears would rise in my eyes because it was all so very beautiful.

But it was not to be. Father and Mother together with the kids left shortly after eleven pm to be sure to get a good seat – a seat from which one could see the altar instead of being stuck behind the broad face of a marbled column. I left about thirty minutes later; there was always room at the gallery for choir members. I shut the apartment door and went downstairs. To my horror, I found the outside door locked. Father had said he would leave it open, but either someone from the building had come in after he left, or else the night watchman had locked it up from outside. Now I could not go to church, but neither could I get back into the apartment. I was trapped in the stairway. I could have screamed with rage. The only remedy was to ask one of the tenants to help me out; but at near midnight I did not feel free to bother anyone. I was condemned to spend our wonderful, once a year, divine midnight mass locked in a cold and empty stairway. Thanks to Mother, who wouldn't let me have a key. That would not happen again, I vowed.

After stomping about like a caged animal for a time I settled down on the fourth floor steps. They were the cleanest because least used. I made myself as comfortable as possible and eventually dozed off.

Ilse had gone home for Christmas by train and was to return by Sunday evening. She didn't make it. Monday's mail brought a letter from her that was addressed to Mother. She took it to her bedroom to read. When she came out again her face was hard. "What did Ilse say?" I asked.

"Never you mind," she answered and told me what chores to do.

It seemed that once again a housemaid had run away from Mother. I could see that I would have a real fight on my hands now, almost a fight for my life, and it gripped me with fear. When I did the grocery shopping, Hildi wanted to come along.

"Not today," I said. It came out harshly. Hildi looked hurt, but I couldn't deal with her pain. I had my own to cope with.

Before I did anything else, I went to church. The Christmas decorations were still in place, incense lingered on the air, and silence prevailed. Thoughts, needs, plans, and a million ifs, buts, and ands rambled through my mind like a herd of sheep, straying this way and that. After a while, I felt calmer and was able to focus my thoughts. When I left the church, inwardly strong and resolved, I knew what I had to do. I would play the homemaker for four weeks to give Mother time to find another housemaid. Come February one, I would either work in the office or leave town.

"What took you so long?" Mother said in her harsh, suspicious way when I returned. Instantly, and fairly automatic, I shot back as I walked past her, "I give you four weeks to find another housemaid. Then I'll work in the office or leave town."

Once said, I realized the brazenness of my answer. But I didn't care. Yet I couldn't believe that Mother would just take it without objection, without punishment, without even a word. I took the groceries into the kitchen and started lunch. Not until Mother went downstairs was I able to let go of the fear that she would come in any moment now to confront me with a wooden clothes hanger. She would hold it tightly in her right fist, pressed against the side of her body as though to endow it with extra power from her own hard, corseted tightness. When Hildi came in and looked at me, searching my face for evidence of my inner disposition, I said with a smile, "all's well with the world." She smiled back. Hildi could never hold a grudge.

While Father was watching the news, during a convenient moment I told him of my plan. He looked to Mother. Mother stared at the television and said nothing. I couldn't tell if she had heard. I didn't wait for a reaction from either one and went to write a letter to Leon. Then I wrote to Steffi, telling her that I didn't expect her parents to keep the job open for me because I was still not sure what would happen.

Next day, I had house and apartment keys made for myself and ordered a post office box where I could receive my mail. Then I went to see Father about the money he owed me. He was looking through the morning's mail when I came in. When he looked up, I told him that I had come for my money. Father could be very funny. He pulled a few coins from his pocket, and with a look of utmost sincerity he showed them to me and said, "will that be enough?" I laughed. Father grinned sheepishly.

"No, Dad, that's not enough," I said.

"You might as well have your savings book."

"What savings book?"

"The one I started for you after you graduated."

"That sounds good. Can I have it right now?"

"Later. It's in my desk upstairs."

Father kept his word. I couldn't help wondering what had prompted him to agree. My own show of firmness? To buy me to stay with Mother? Or maybe he had noticed that I needed new clothes. That, however, seemed unlikely because Father was not the type to notice anything about the females in his life. On the contrary, he was used to being attended to by us. Perhaps he simply thought it time that I learn to manage money.

My savings book showed a greater balance than I had expected. By some inexplicable law of ownership, though, mere planning the use of it made it drift away very quickly. While I first just wanted to pay my debts and maybe buy a new dress, suddenly, I also needed new shoes and a sweater, then some make-up, some fancy underwear and nylons, chocolate of course, and a pretty new dress for Hildi who had never worn anything but hand-me-downs. Before I knew it, temptation to pay the Railroad Mission not right now but later became a bone of contention between duty and desire. I paid off Mother first. When I handed her the money she said, "next time you run away, don't bother to come back."

School started again on Monday after Epiphany, which is celebrated on January sixth. It began to snow the following day, and by afternoon it lay thick and fluffy everywhere that neither people nor vehicles presumed to trespass. I took the little boys sledding in the castle park. Two long natural ramps, which had once been created for royal coach approaches to the Orangerie's grand entry, made a perfect incline for sledding. A few more days of very low temperatures made it possible for Hans and Hildi to ice skate in the same park on an artificially created ice rink out in the open. It was safer than the park's pond, which rarely froze solid enough to skate on.

I did the usual chores, did homework with the children, and watched Mother for signs of hiring a new housemaid. Walter was away in Munich again, but Paula and Werner came by on Sunday afternoons for coffee. Paula, now safe out of Mother's reach, liked to needle her with comments about her own past treatment at Mother's hands. "I should have been your housemaid instead of your daughter, then I could have run away too," she said one time.

"Just wait till you have a house full of children," Mother replied sweetly with affected tenderness. With her head slightly bowed and her eyes in a sideways glance, she appeared like a humble sinner who is taking his just punishment. At the sound of the word children, Paula looked to Werner, her mouth opened as though she meant to say something, but she didn't.

"So, Fanny is helping out again, huh?"

"Yep, till the end of the month," I said firmly. "Till Mother finds a new housemaid."

"What happens if she doesn't find one?" Paula asked, looking from me to Mother and back.

"I don't know," I answered. "Come February one, I work in the office or leave."

Paula looked at me, utterly astonished. Mother stared down on her plate. Father and Werner were wrangling over politics.

"Help me with the dishes," I said to Paula. Once in the kitchen, Paula said, "no, really, what are you going to do if Mother doesn't get another housemaid?"

"Just as I told you. I'll work in the office or leave."

"Leave? Where to?"

"Munich or Wiesenthal. I actually have two choices." I couldn't help but gloat about the fact. "But it's not that simple. I have the awful feeling that any moment now, she's going to wake up to what I've been saying. Then she'll give the broomstick a workout on my legs. Have you ever tried to do your own thing?"

"Yep. Just once. She slapped me so hard that my glasses went flying and I had to get a new pair. But what about working in the office?"

"Dad told me that I could after vacation is over. I'll wait until the end of the month, though. Don't you think that's fair?"

"Mother doesn't care about fair."

"I know that," I said. "I mean that it's fair of me to give her time to find a new maid. Then, if she hasn't got one, and I haven't noticed her doing anything about it, I don't have to blame myself for leaving her in the lurch."

"Well, I'm just glad I'm out of it," Paula said with a sigh of relief and turned to go back to the dining room. Just then, I remembered the look on Paula's face when Mother mentioned children. I figured that Paula was pregnant.

I poked her in the butt as she headed out the door. "Pregnant?" I asked.

She turned with a look of surprise, annoyance even. "Why do you say that?"

"Just a wild guess."

"I don't want anybody to know yet," she said.

I hadn't had any experience with pregnancy moods and dispositions, but I certainly could tell that Paula was not pleased. "Don't tell anybody," she whispered to me, turned and went back to the dining room. Mother was just giving Werner a lecture about the virtues of being a frugal business owner.

Mother made no signs of looking for a housemaid. She was fairly pleasant, even genial at times. The closer we got to February, though, the more nervous I became. I had thought myself to be ever so much in control of my life now, but my body was still reacting the old way – with fear and sickening tension.

On the first day of February I got up as usual, tended to the kids, then went downstairs to Father's office. He looked up and seemed surprised to see me.

"It's the first of February and I'm ready to work in the office."

"I don't know," Father said haltingly, and irritation wrinkled up his forehead. He looked around his desk as if a job was hidden there among his papers. When he couldn't find one, he looked up and said, "I suppose you could help Frau Raabe with the filing."

"And what do I do after that?"

"I'm not sure. We'll have to find something."

"Dad, do you have a proper job for me or not?"

"Not really. Not right now, anyway."

Right about then, the phone rang, and from the way Father answered it, I knew it was Mother.

"Your Mother needs you upstairs," he said as he hung up, obviously relieved. It was a real blow. Father had no clue what he was doing to me.

"You told me I could work in the office," I said, trying hard to stay calm in the face of this betrayal. "You knew I was counting on it." And with my mind getting ready for the inevitable, I added, "at least give me the money that you owe me for last month's work."

Father looked surprised but reached into his billfold and gave me whatever cash he had on him. It was more than enough for a train ticket to Wiesenthal. "What are you going to do?" Father called after me as I left his office. I didn't answer. Out in the stairway I stopped to collect myself. I could not afford to cry now; I had to be strong because the moment of truth was nearing.

Mother was waiting with instructions for me. After she went downstairs I had time to think about what to do. I could go to Munich. Leon had told me in a letter that his brother's butchery could use me as a sales clerk. But I was not keen about working among butchers. They kill animals.

Steffi's parents had hired someone for their office, but I knew I was welcome anyway. I should go there. I'd have a sister to live with, and it might even be fun and perhaps more satisfying to find a job on my own. But how to say good-bye to the boys, and to Hildi! Could I simply walk away from her? Should I, could I, just leave without saying a word to Mother and Father?

I went to do the grocery shopping and errands, utterly wretched inside. The weather was wet and dreary – a perfect match for my disposition. Sitting and thinking in my church did not help this time. On my way to the post office, I came near Paula's home. I went to see her, not really knowing what for. Perhaps I would ask her to look after Hildi for me when I was gone. As I entered the shop, Werner was just finished with a customer while Paula was busy with another one.

"Just in time," he called to me.

"In time for what?" I asked.

"I need help in the office, and you want a job, I hear."

"I sure do," I replied and sat down on a chair to think about this unexpected opportunity. The day looked much better already. Werner filled me in on the details. The work would be just what I was looking for; the hours would be from eight to one. The pay was more than I expected in my ignorance of payroll matters, and best of all, I would still be able to look after the children in the afternoons.

On my way home, though, I began to have second thoughts. There was something about Werner that struck me, something for which I had no name and couldn't define. But whatever it was, it made me feel uncomfortable. Did I really want to be near him for five hours every day? Once Paula had the baby, I would probably be there all day. And I would still have to face and be around Mother every day. She would not let me go to work for someone else so easily She would have all sorts of things for me to do before going to work, she would never care about my responsibility to someone else, never allowing me to determine when and how much time I would spend in her service. It would be a constant battle.

I was late, very late, getting back with the groceries. Since I had my own key, Mother didn't notice me until I entered the kitchen. "Where were you? Running the streets like a bitch in heat," it spewed maliciously from her mouth, and she slapped me across the face. I was stunned.

"That's it," I yelled. "Now I'm leaving. Werner offered me a part-time job; I was going to take it and I would have been home to look after the kids for you. But not anymore." I headed for the kitchen door, but Mother planted herself in front of it.

"You'll do nothing of the sort. Get busy with the potatoes." Her eyes were wide and threatening, her lips pulled taut against her teeth. In her right hand, pressed against her side, she held a wooden clothes hanger that had my name on it. Resolved not to let this temporary setback stop me, I began peeling potatoes. Mother busied herself with the meat. The tension between us was thick enough to cut with a knife.

After lunch, the kids settled down to do their homework. Hildi seemed restless, and she kept looking at me as though she sensed something. "You know something, don't you," I said.

She searched my face; it seemed to me that she was reading my mind. "You're going to leave again, aren't you," she said mournfully.

"Oh Hildi!" I felt the tears rising in my eyes at the thought of all the things this child, so sensitive, might be feeling and yet have no one to tell it to.

"What does she know?" Hans asked. He hadn't heard the first part of our exchange.

"Fanny is leaving again," Hildi said.

"Why are you leaving, Fanny?" Markus wanted to know.

"Yeah, why?" Matthias chimed in.

"Oh, it's a long story. I don't think you'd understand."

"What's there to understand?" Hans said. "You want to work in the office, right? I thought you were doing that now."

"Father has no job for me and Mother wants me to stay and be the housemaid."

"We want you to stay and be the housemaid, too," the little boys said in unison.

"But I learned to do office work and want to do that."

"Don't you like taking care of us?" Markus asked.

"Oh, of course I do. That's why a part-time job with Werner would have been ideal. Then I could spend the afternoons with you. But Mother…"

"Won't let you," said Hans.

"I wonder how it will be with me, when I'm eighteen," Hildi said with a sour grimace.

"I'll be gone, then, and you'll be the eldest," said Hans.

"Yeah! And you'll be our babysitter then," Matthias said.

"I'm so sorry, guys, but I have no other choice but to leave. Now listen to me: Hans, you need to look after Hildi and help her with her homework because Mother doesn't have enough patience, you hear?" Hans nodded. "And you two," I said, pointing at Markus and Mathias, "you need to behave real good so that Mother doesn't get angry and let it out on someone else. You'll soon have a new housemaid because Mother really wants to be in the store. Ilse was o.k., wasn't she?"

"Well, she was better than Mother, that's for sure," replied Hans. "But the next one won't stay long either, and then it'll be back to having Mother around all the time again. Not much fun."

"Well, maybe next time you're in luck and you'll get someone who's real sweet and loves kids and knows how to get along with Mother. It could happen, right?"

"Sure, why not," admitted Hans.

I was glad to have talked with the kids about my leaving. They took it better than I expected. Sometime during the evening, the little boys talked about it in Mother's presence. She gave me a look of warning and said, "remember, the next time you run away you don't need to come back."

"I'm not running away," I replied and added with emphasis, "I'm going away." It felt good to be planning an orderly exit instead of beating a hasty retreat.

On the following morning, I said good-bye to the kids who were leaving for school. Hildi cried and hugged me a long time until Hans pried her lose. He shook my hand like an adult and wished me good luck. Perhaps he realized the importance of being the eldest in the home now. I packed what bags I had, and then went to the bathroom. When I came back, the clothes I had packed were strewn across my bed and the bags were gone. It felt so utterly hateful, this deed, that it made me cry. Alright, I thought, I'll take nothing with me, rather like starting a new life without old baggage.

I got dressed in a couple of outfits, stuffed whatever clean underwear I could into my coat pockets and handbag, and went downstairs to say good-bye to Father.

"What do you mean?" he asked.

"I'm leaving Dad. I'm going to Wiesenthal. You don't have a job for me. Werner had a part-time job for me and I would have taken it, but Mother…" I had trouble to keep from crying.

"Mother needs you," Father said.

"She needs somebody to control and yell at," I said. "Do you know what she calls me? She calls me a bitch in heat. What do you think of that?"

Father was quiet for a moment. Then he begged me to change my mind, used guilt about leaving Mother without help, used the boys and Hildi to make me feel bad for leaving them, and pointed out to me that I was not yet of age and wouldn't be until I turned twenty-one.

"What about how she treats me?" I nearly yelled.

"Oh, you never cared," he said and stood up. He was angry now. "Like the night when Matthias was born: you didn't care enough to get up." He started pacing.

"I was asleep!"

"Paula called you!"

"But I didn't wake up enough to really hear!" Father just shrugged. "Well, I didn't want to run away again, that's why I came to say good-bye to you. I packed my bags, but while I was in the bathroom Mother threw my things out and took away the bags. I have nothing but the few clothes that I'm wearing." Father, as usual, had no comments about Mother's actions.

"Well, remember where you come from," he finally said with resignation. Then he reached in his billfold, pulled out some money and gave it to me. "Let me know how you're doing," he said. Then we shook hands and I left.

I found a job as a receptionist in the office of Dr. Merton, a Gynecologist. His practice was on the street level of his townhouse, a neo-classical building from the turn of the century. It might have been considered beautiful without the wartime shell-shots that looked like the frazzled edges of some giant drill bit at work. Dr. Merton lived with his wife and three children on the second floor. Two apartments on the third floor and the attic were rented out.

The building grounds included a small front yard, the width of the building and about ten feet deep. It was surrounded by black wrought iron fencing with a gate across the walkway that lead to the front door. Attractive wrought iron grating, bulging outward to allow for flowerboxes, adorned and protected the street-level windows. A prominent white sign on the wall beside the door announced in large black letters the practice of Dr. Merton. On the doorjamb were located small nameplates with adjacent doorbells, one for each apartment.

Dr. Merton was a middle-aged man with pink cheeks and graying hair on a large, broad head. His jowls and girth betrayed a heavy eater; his hands were short, his fingers fat and repulsive. He was a kind, friendly man, soft-spoken and non-demanding, almost nurturing - a real blessing for a novice at a new job like me. My desk stood near one of three windows in the large reception area that was also the waiting room. I answered the telephone, welcomed patients, readied patient files for the doctor and did all the filing. From time to time Dr. Merton dictated a letter in his office, which also functioned as the exam room. I took the dictation in shorthand and then typed it. Taking dictation was a real challenge because the Doctor spoke very fast. There were lots of lengthy Latin terms I had never heard before and had a hard time deciphering afterward. Sometimes, after hours, he used the Dictaphone for dictation. At times, he wanted an additional carbon copy but didn't mention it until the very end. That meant typing the whole thing over again. When I got nervous I made a lot of typing errors, and then I had to carefully erase the single mistaken letter without disturbing the neighboring ones, then try to line up the error spot accurately to type over it, and then do the same thing on each copy. It was awful.

The doctor usually had a room full of patients waiting and could not get away for a break. Instead, his wife brought him a small pot of coffee and some fresh pastry from the neighborhood bakery during mid-morning. Frau Merton was a short, matronly woman, and chubby like her husband. People were indulging their appetites now that years of near-starvation diets during and immediately following the war had ended.

Being new at this job took a lot of concentration, and many a night I fell into bed exhausted. I was in no mood, then to listen to Steffi's days at school and play. Steffi had a boyfriend, Klaus, and she was eager to talk about him. She wasn't so eager to hear me talking about the women patients at the clinic, though. They were sick, of course, often in pain and anxious about their conditions. Sometimes, the wait for their turn was long, then their frustration was vented on me. Some older patients seemed to think of me as totally inconsequential, and in a way they were right, because I was not the doctor. It took all the courage I had to stand my ground in the face of such women.

And so the days passed quickly and quietly. I paid a small amount of my income to Frau Rhein as a share in expenses, and Steffi and I either shared or alternated chores. Hildi and I kept in touch via occasional telephone calls. Leon and I kept in touch via mail, and one day I received a letter in which he asked if he could come to visit me at Easter. I wasted no time inviting him after Frau Rhein assured me that he was welcome.

"Oh, you'll have your lover boy here, all to your little old self, huh?" Steffi teased.

"Yeah! And you'll have your lover boy here all to your little old self, too, huh?"

"Why don't we do something together," Steffi said. "I know, we could go see a movie together, all four of us, or maybe a dance. I'll have to find out if there's a dance anywhere. Of course not on Holy Friday, or Saturday. Maybe there'd be one on Easter Sunday. I'll ask Mom!"

"I'm pretty sure that no dances are held on a day like Easter," said Frau Rhein with an indulging smile. "You can always go see a movie, though. Or we could take a drive in the country. What do you think?"

"Nah, that's boring," said Steffi, and I was glad that she had said it, because I felt the same way. "We'll go see a movie. Or maybe we'll just wait for the guys to get here; maybe they have a good idea."

"I'm sure they do," said Frau Rhein with a laugh.

"I can't wait to meet Klaus," I said to Steffi. "What's he like?"

"Oh, he's soo good-looking! Taller than I, has thick dark hair, and he plays the violin too. That's actually how I met him. We take classes from the same teacher. Oh, I told you about him when you came the last time, remember? I had only seen him then, but one time, after you had left, our lessons were cancelled and we ran into each other. He's a couple of years older than me. It's his second year at the University. And that's the problem; I can only see him during breaks."

"And your parents already invite him to their house!" I was utterly astonished that such generosity should exist.

"Well, they think of him as a friend. A friend who happened to be a boy, see?"

"And is that how you think of him?"

"Well, not exactly," Steffi revealed with lowered voice and a glance to the door to make sure it was shut. "I'm really crazy about this guy. And I think he likes me too. He even kissed me!"

"Wow! Isn't that a bit pushy?"

"No! That's just the way it is with us. And I was thinking – I know I said we should do something together, but I've changed my mind about that. We should leave together, but then I want Klaus and me to split. I bet you'd much rather be alone with Leon, too, wouldn't you?"

"Sounds good to me."

"But you'd have to cover for me."

"Oh Steffi, I don't know about that!"

"You're my friend, aren't you?"

"Yes, of course, but I can't lie to your parents."

"What's there to lie? We leave together and come back together. They never need to know that we split up."

"What if something unexpected happens?"

"Like what?"

"Well, I don't know. Something. Anything. We better talk about this some more," I said, feeling doomed to fall into a trap from which I would not come out as clean as I went in. Steffi had come a long way since the days when she was timid and easily frightened. She used to carry herself as though she feared getting hit over the head. She had stopped talking about her psychic ability. Perhaps she had decided to suppress it; probably because of the fear and anxiety her visions had caused her. I couldn't really blame her. Seeing something bad happening to someone and not being able to help ought to be pretty painful. Even doing something about it, as we did in the case of Erna, turned out to be pretty painful when she died anyway. Now that Steffi pursued music at the high school instead of wrestling with dull business courses in Venusbrunn, she had become much more confident.

"What'll you do when you graduate next year?" I asked her one evening.

"I'll be studying music at the University."

"The same one as Klaus?"

"Of course, dummy," she said, and with her fist hit me on the arm.

"Ouch! That hurt!" And I hit her back.

"And what are you going to do with the rest of your life? Sit in an office and get nagged by sick old women?" she asked.

"You know, I don't know about this office work. I don't think it's the right job for me. Of course I'm happy to have it right now, don't get me wrong. But the only people I meet are crotchety old women. I mean, there are some young women, too, but it's the old ones that are so bothersome. And there's nobody my age anywhere around."

"Well, you'll have to do something else, then."

"What?"

"Well, I don't know. That's up to you."

"My parents never talk about my future, Hans' or Hildi's neither." Then I remembered something. "Wait. I did have an idea once. I used to think I want to be a governess."

"A governess," Steffi repeated with a prissy voice. "You'd be taking care of other people's kids. You already did that, with your own siblings."

"But there's more to it than that. I'd be totally in charge of children whose parents are on the go a lot. I'd be teaching them, too, almost like school. And if the whole family travels, I'd be going too."

"Actually, I think you'd be good at it."

"I had completely forgotten about it."

"Well, now you remember. So do something about it."

"Oh, you have no idea what you're saying. I'd have to go to some school, and my parents would have to pay for it. My Mother would never allow it!"

"Well, what about your Father? Would he allow it?"

"I have no idea. I had completely forgotten about being a Governess. Maybe now that I know... I'll have to think about it." After the events of the past few months, I thought, perhaps there was a chance. I felt something very unusual cropping up inside me, vision and hope, as if a door or window had suddenly opened in that dead end wall I had faced for too long, to reveal choices and opportunities.

"I think dinner is ready," Steffi said and got up. I followed her to the dining room. After dinner we did the dishes and cleaned up the kitchen. Herr Rhein let me choose a TV program that he and Frau Rhein happened to like also, but Steffi was doomed to do homework.

Leon arrived during early evening of Holy Saturday. It was April, and the weather had turned a little warmer and the buds on some of the trees had begun to open. Leon knew the way from the railroad station, and when the downstairs doorbell rang I went to open it for him. He came in, set down his bag, and without saying a word he put his arms around me and pulled me close to himself and held me. Oh, how I had longed for this moment, this embrace, so gentle and loving, so strong and protective, like a Father's. And the sudden realization of what I hadn't received from my Father overwhelmed me, and I cried tears of pain and sorrow while Leon stroked me gently and waited.

"Feel better now?" he asked with a smile, when I reached for a handkerchief in my pocket.

"Oh, what a man you are," I whispered. And Leon kissed my wet eyes.

"What took you so long?" Steffi asked with a grin as we came upstairs. Seeing my tear smeared face though, she decided to wait with further questions. Herr Rhein was in the living room reading a paper. He got up and shook hands with Leon. "Good to see you again, Herr Kramer," he said. "Did you have a good trip?"

"Yes, thank you, Herr Rhein. The train was pretty crowded, but I guess that's to be expected at this time of the year."

"We will have supper in a short while. Will you join us?"

"Yes, thank you very much. But I'd like to wash up first."

"Of course. You know the way? Steffi set another plate. Oh, I guess you know." Then looking at me and seeing my red eyes, he teased, "oh, poor Stef. She cried tears of joy."

I went to hide in the kitchen and help Frau Rhein. She took a long look at me and my red eyes and said with a smile of approval, "Leon came, huh? He's a fine young man." Steffi set the table, and pretty soon we sat down together to eat.

Leon spent the night in the hostel and picked me up for mass Easter morning. He was dressed in his best suit, tie, and white shirt. Frau Rhein offered him breakfast, but he declined since he wanted to receive Holy Communion. Wiesenthal's church was a post-war building, plain, straight, almost sinister in its starkness, and lacking all of the wonderful eye-catching artwork I was used to seeing and feeling in my own parish church. But Leon's presence felt so good, I didn't mind the ugly church.

After mass we went to a café to have coffee and a breakfast roll with butter and jam while he was telling me about his work at his brother's butcher shop.

"Do you like your work? Who actually kills the animals?" I had wanted to ask this for a long time.

"I do, every butcher does. It's what I have to do. And, no, I don't exactly like it. But I also cook sausage, and people really like my sausages. That makes me feel good."

"Yes, but you also kill animals."

" I didn't really want to be a butcher, but there were no carpenters around who would take on an apprentice. Too many masters in all sorts of professions got killed during the war, so when I finished eighth grade, I took what I could get. Anything to learn a trade and earn a living.

"Would you change it if you could?"

"Oh, there's no way I could do that."

"Well if you could, would you?"

"I never thought about it," he said with a far-away look in his eyes. "Yes, maybe I would. I always liked woodworking, or carpentry. It's great to be able to build something, something beautiful that will last, maybe even for generations," he said with a wistful smile. But then he turned to me and asked, "do you like your job?"

"Yes, pretty much. I mean, Dr. Merton is a nice man, and very patient. He never makes me feel bad when I make a mistake. But I don't really do anything very important. Nothing very exciting. I answer the phone, keep the files, and type a few letters, but nothing really important, you know?"

"Yes, I know what you mean. Like making sausage. Oh sure, it tastes good, but after its eaten, what do you have? Nothing. You don't even need it to live."

"Steffi said something the other day that reminded me that I once wanted to be a Governess. What do you think?"

"A Governess. Sounds like an important, and maybe even prestigious, job."

"The more I think about it, the more I think I'll talk to my Dad about it some day. Maybe you should think about changing your job, too."

"Oh, there's no way," Leon said as though I had asked him to introduce me to the Pope. "I'm working toward a Master now. Do you know what it would mean to switch? Three years of apprenticeship, if I could even find a Master to take me on, two years as journeyman, and then some more time for a Master. My income would be cut drastically. I'll be twenty-four in August. If I changed jobs, I could be thirty by the time I'm finished."

"Well, it was just a thought," I said, almost sorry I mentioned it. But he took my hand and looked into my eyes and smiled.

"I think you care about me," he said.

"I like you a lot, Leon. You're the best thing that ever happened to me." Leon caressed my hands with his lips and it sent shivers of joy down my spine.

We talked for a long time, walked and talked, and it seemed that we could never find an end. The politics of the day lent an earthy flavor to our conversations. Chancellor Konrad Adenauer was running for re-election on the promise to never accept East Germany, under the control and occupation of the Soviet Union, as a separate state. Leon's Family had come from those Eastern regions, and a win for Adenauer's opponent could mean the end of their dream to go back to their homeland.

We got back in time for dinner. Klaus had arrived while we were out. He was tall and dark-haired the way Steffi had described. He was also very handsome, but there was something in his demeanor that I didn't like. Herr Rhein engaged him in a discussion of federal politics. Klaus, when asked a question, would raise his head, look rather loftily about and answer almost above the questioner's head. His speech was loud and measured then, as if he tried to convince himself that things were the way he said they are. Steffi adored him, it was plain to see. And her adoration seemed to feed his conviction that he was just about the best thing that ever happened to a girl. He nearly dominated the conversation at dinner, causing her parents to glance at each other from time to time with a look of amused alarm. Frau Rhein, especially, kept a close eye on Steffi, and her expression, at first friendly and carefree, became one of concern.

Eventually, the conversation turned to plans for the afternoon. Klaus and Steffi had plenty of time, but Leon's return train to Munich left shortly after five pm and I would go with him to the station. Eventually, we settled for a bus ride to the Castle on the outskirts of town. It had been the summer residence of the local aristocracy. After the war it became a museum and a café. The park-like grounds and small woods were an ideal place for a Sunday stroll. When Herr Rhein offered to drive us there, Steffi declined, with a look to me that requested complicity. I agreed.

Steffi and I hurried to do the dishes after dinner, while her parents probed Klaus. On leaving the apartment, Frau Rhein said that we should stay together, and return together. We all agreed. I started worrying.

"Oh, I almost forgot," said Frau Rhein to me. "Your sister called. She wants you to call her back."

"Hildi called?"

"No, it was your sister Paula. She left her phone number for you," and with that, Frau Rhein handed me a hand-written note. I was perplexed. Why would Paula call? Was somebody very sick? Did someone die? Did she have her baby? I kept staring at the paper and asking, as if Frau Rhein had the answer if I would just ask the right question. Finally, Leon took my hand and pulled me out the door behind Steffi and Klaus.

Klaus had his arm wrapped around Steffi's neck in a possessive, controlling sort of way that, it seemed to me, could be uncomfortably tight for her. She didn't seem to care or notice, though. Her right hand gripped his right hand, which dangled down across her chest, and her left arm was wrapped around his waist. She looked up to him adoringly. When we turned the corner of the block, Steffi stopped, and turning to Leon and me she said, "you two go ahead. We might do something else."

"Your mother said for us to stay together, Steffi," I reminded her. The guys were silent.

"I know, I know…"

"You're going to get yourself and me in trouble."

"Oh Fannie, don't be so glum, "we're just going our own way for a while and then we'll meet someplace. How about right over there, at that fountain. What time?"

"We'd have to meet at about five pm to give Leon enough time to make it to the station, right, Leon?"

"Yes, five is good."

"Steffi, I don't like this. What if something goes wrong and you'll be late?"

"Nothing will go wrong."

"Accidents do happen, you know. Klaus, what do you say? Her parents said for us to stay together and we agreed."

77

"Nothing is going to happen," he said in his superior way. "We'll be back here by five."

"By the way, we don't know which bus to take to the castle. Maybe we just better not go there either. I'd worry about being late." And turning to Leon, I added, "let's just go walking and exploring the neighborhood. I haven't had much of a chance to do that. Do you want to?"

"Whatever you like is fine with me," said Leon. I put my arm in his and after all four of us synchronized our watches, we split up and went in different directions.

I kept thinking about the phone call. Long distance was expensive, and one would only call about very important matters. Well, it would have to wait until evening. Leon and I came to the city castle grounds and ambled along the paths that separated and grouped lawns, flowerbeds, and fountains. It had rained the night before and the paths were muddy, so we headed back to the pavement and found a little Café where we had coffee and cake.

"Last year, we couldn't get together for our birthdays," Leon said. "Maybe we can make it work this year."

"Oh yes, for sure. But are you saying we won't see each other again until August? That's four months. Oh, I don't want to wait that long."

"Well, I could come up again between now and then. Or you could come to Munich. I'd love to show you the city. I think you'd like it. It has a kind of easy-going atmosphere like a small town - Like Hanfurt - but it's much bigger, of course, and it has an international flair."

"I'll have to save up some money first. I had to buy some clothes. You know, I left Hanfurt with nothing but the clothes on my back. Did I ever tell you that I actually put on three outfits on top of each other? Underwear and stockings I stuffed into my coat pockets. I must have looked awfully fat and lumpy."

"You could still work for my brother, you know. And he still has a spare room. We would see each other every day," Leon said.

"Oh, I couldn't. Killing animals... I can't help but feel that they know when they're being butchered. They've got to suffer real fear. It's getting so I don't even care to eat meat anymore, because every time I bite into it I think about biting into a live animal."

"It's that bad, huh?"

"I wish you could do something else."

Leon was quiet then. I felt that I had reached a dead-end. I did not like butchery, but it was unreasonable to expect Leon to change his profession. And why should he. To please me? Why? We weren't married. We weren't even engaged to be married. I had no right to ask him to change.

On the way to the fountain where we were to meet Klaus and Steffi, neither one of us said very much. We sat down on the stone bench that surrounded the fountain as part of it. Leon put his arm around my back, and so we waited, quietly, overshadowed by the disturbed harmony of our moods. The neighborhood protestant church steeple rang four forty-five.

"Sounds just like the church near your house."

"Oh, how we used to walk up and down that street. How we talked. And every time that church clock struck and reminded me that it was time to break it up I'd get that awful sick feeling in my stomach."

"If you come to Munich, we can go dancing any time you want," Leon said

"Oh, I 'd love that."

I was getting nervous. Steffi was nowhere in sight, and I had no idea where to look for her. What on earth would I tell her parents if she didn't show up pretty soon. When the clock struck five, Leon said, "I need to get going."

"Darn it. What am I going to do? Lie to her parents, or give Steffi away? How can she do that to me."

"I tell you what: I'll go upstairs, take my bag and say good-bye. If they ask I'll tell them you're waiting downstairs to take me to the station."

"You mean just me, or all of us?"

"Just you. If they ask I'll tell them what happened. I can't be blamed for Steffi taking off on her own, and you won't have to lie for her."

"Oh Leon, you are marvelous!" I kissed him on the cheek.

We came to the house, I waited downstairs and Leon went inside. A few moments later he came out with his bag. "They asked," he said with a significant look.

"Poor Steffi."

Leon took me by the hand. Neither one of us said much on the way to the station, as if everything we wanted to say, or plan, or resolve was too much to deal with in the few minutes we had left together. The train had already pulled in. We hurried to the platform, Leon wrapped himself around me one more time, kissed me on the cheek, gave me one last long look with glowing eyes, and then he climbed aboard. The conductor blew the whistle, walked along the train and shut whatever doors had been left open, then the train set in motion. Leon waved from his window and I waved back for as long as I could see him.

Not knowing when I would see Leon again made me feel sad. The Rheins were good to me, the doctor was good to me, and Steffi was a good friend to me. But my day to day existence with them felt like the light of a new moon, while being with Leon felt like warm brilliant sunshine in a glorious flower garden. Leon had spoiled me. My tears flowed again.

I wandered about, thinking not only about Leon but also about Steffi and what she might have gotten herself into. I needed to figure out what to do or say to her and her parents. When I finally showed up around seven, Steffi came downstairs to open the door. Her face was smeared with tears. She said nothing, just turned around and ran upstairs. The Rheins were in the living room. I thought I better get things over with and went in, said, "good evening" and sat down on a chair.

Frau Rhein said, "we know what happened. It's not your fault that Steffi decided to go off by herself with Klaus, so don't feel bad about it. If you're hungry, help yourself. You know where the kitchen is." She smiled at me and I felt relieved. Then I remembered Paula's phone call and I asked permission to call her back. The telephone was located in the hallway. I dialed, and Paula answered the phone.

"Paula, its me, Stephanie. What happened? Why did you call? How did you get this number?"

"Easy, Sis, first things first. I got your number from Hildi, and I'm calling because I want to ask your help. Guess what?"

"Guess what? What? Somebody sick?"

"No, no. Nothing like that."

"I don't know. Come on, tell me. I'm using the Rhein's phone. Make it short."

"I'm going to have twins!"

"Twins! Wow! When?"

"July fifteen."

"Twins! Oh my goodness! Are you excited?

"Well, yes and no. It's going to be a lot of work, and that's why I called. I'll need help when I bring them home from the hospital. Maybe even sooner. I'm already pretty big and uncomfortable. The doctor says I might have them early. But either way, I really need some help. Werner's mother is absolutely useless. She doesn't have a clue. Had one child, and that was a hundred years ago. So Mother thought maybe I could get you to come and help."

"Mother, huh?"

"Interesting, isn't it."

"What about Father! What was his reaction?"

"Oh, he's all for it too, for you to come and help, I mean."

"Oh Paula, I have to think about that. I have a nice job here, you know, with a Gynecologist. He's very good to me and I don't know that I would want to give it up. And besides, I get paid."

"Well, you'll get paid here too. Werner will pay you something. Think about it. Whatever you decide I'll have to accept, I guess. Can't force you. But do think about it. I know you like babies."

"I do, I do. Okay, I'll think about it. Say hi to Hildi and the boys for me, okay? Bye now." I hung up, deep in thought. As I entered Steffi's and my room, she sat up from her bed.

"Nothing's going to happen, huh?" I said.

"Oh Stef, I'm so sorry."

"So, what did happen?"

"Oh, it's pretty bad. First we just went walking. He showed me where he lives, and then he took me inside his apartment. His parents weren't home, but he hadn't told me that. He showed me his room, and his collection of opera albums, then we had some wine and he became, well, he started kissing me really hard, you know?"

"Oh yes, I know," I said in memory of a tall seventeen year old who had me so tightly in his grip that I couldn't get away. I had ended up with frazzled lips for which I had to invent an explanation which, I feared, nobody believed. "They develop amazing strength, don't they."

"Yeah! And you know, I was getting worried that he would rape me."

"Oh, poor Steffi."

"Well, I didn't want him to be like that, and I managed to push him away. He got mad at me, and I was afraid I'd lose him, but I didn't want to... oh, it was awful."

"And then?"

"Well, all of a sudden it was past five and I jumped up and started running. Klaus just sat there; he didn't care at all," and Steffi started crying again. "I'm not going to see him anymore."

"I should hope not."

"But he's so cute!"

"Yea, but do you need a cute rapist in your life?"

Steffi shook her head. The way she sat there, on her bed, her head hanging and her dark hair falling into her face she looked just as helpless and fragile as she used to during Venusbrunn days. I grabbed her by the hands, pulled her up and hugged her. "Poor Steffi."

"Yes, poor me," she said, wiped her tears and blew her nose. "I finally have a boy friend and he turns out to be a jerk!"

"How come you didn't look at him with your psychic vision? You could have seen what he's like in his aura."

"I don't know. I stopped doing that."

"How come?"

"Oh, I don't know. Maybe it was just too much to handle."

"I don't get it."

"Well, I didn't like being so different. It made me feel so, so like an alien almost. Not that I know what an alien would feel like," she said with a grin. "But I could never talk about what I saw and heard: bad things, good things, things that nobody else saw or heard. I mean, I used to tell you about it and you listened, but then I left Venusbrunn and since then I never knew anybody I could trust. So, I figured it's safer to just not see and hear."

"And you can turn if off, just like that?"

"Well, I figured if I could see, then I could also not see if I didn't want to. And it worked."

"But aren't you suppressing something that's part of you, like a talent?"

"I don't think so."

"Wouldn't it be just like not playing the violin?"

"No, not at all. I like music, but I don't like this psycho thing."

"Maybe it's because you never knew what to do with it. If somebody had given you a violin when you were just four, you wouldn't have known what to do with that either."

"I suppose."

"Maybe you should talk to that clairvoyant lady, Judith. She'll know what to do."

"Yeah, maybe."

"You want to know something? I'm starving. I need something to eat. Did you have any supper?"

"Could you make me a sandwich?"

"Sure. By the way, what did your parents say when you came back late, and alone?"

"Oh, it was pretty simple. They were annoyed with me, but when I told them that I wouldn't see Klaus anymore they seemed satisfied. I guess they could see from my face that something went wrong."

I went to the kitchen to fix sandwiches, and when I came back I told Steffi what my sister Paula had asked me to do. Steffi thought it would be great to take care of babies. It certainly would be more fun than dealing with crotchety old women or erasing typos. I could see Hildi and the boys, and Mother wouldn't have much say in my work as a proper

Nanny. Nanny! I hadn't thought about being a Nanny. That was almost as good as being a Governess.

My sister Paula had her babies on the seventeenth of June, and one week later I went back to Hanfurt. Ever since I had agreed to be her nanny I hadn't been able to shake some odd feelings about it, not strong enough to get hold of my attention, but there, just below the surface of my awareness. Now, on the train back to Hanfurt, and my mind being unoccupied with duties and responsibilities, I searched out that odd sensation again. Dissecting and analyzing it, it became clear to me that I was happy taking care of babies, that I gladly helped my sister, and that I felt good about seeing the kids again. And, I was very sure that I didn't like being around Werner.

Hildi had asked me via telephone when I would leave Wiesenthal, which train I would take, when it would arrive in Hanfurt. I thought she was just trying to assure herself that my return was more than an empty promise. When I stepped off the train, I suddenly felt myself surrounded, and looking about I discovered my four siblings, smiling, jabbering, hopping up and down. Hildi hugged me, the little boys hugged us, and Hans reached through the human muddle to shake my hand with a grown-up grip. The little ones pressed so close to me that I nearly tripped over them on the way home.

I had played a little game with myself whenever I had returned from Venusbrunn. I pretended to see my hometown, these buildings, sidewalks and trees as if I had never seen them before. And what I saw would confirm and enhance my memories, make them more vivid and enduring. People would walk past me, strangers minding their own business. They would walk through my street, my town, under my trees. They would walk through my memories, and it was alright for them to do so, because their presence was fleeting. It would not jeopardize what was mine alone.

On the way to our apartment on the third floor, we dropped in on Father whose office was on the second floor. "Look what we found!" the kids shouted as we all piled through the door in one big lump. Father looked annoyed at the noise, at first, but then he saw me, and his frown turned into a smile. Father had an unusual smile. The corners of his mouth went down instead of up which made him look bashful or embarrassed.

"Good afternoon," he said in his very formal way, and he reached for my hand. I kissed him on the cheek.

"It's good to be back home, isn't it." he said.

"I don't know yet," I replied. Father frowned. He had expected me to be unhappy anywhere else because in his mind cleaning up after other people had to be a worse thing than cleaning up after one's family. He never knew there was no difference. And that I could be unhappy at home had never sunk in.

Mother had hired a new housemaid; her name was Marlies. She was in her thirties and unmarried. Like Mother, she was tall and sturdy, with a large face that was remarkably ugly. Not a simple kind of homeliness that might have elicited pity or sympathy, but a hard ugly that made one think that her feelings could never be hurt. She came from a village in the Rhoen hills, beautiful country with sparse soil. Her parents had a small farm with two cows and a few pigs. But making a living was hard, and many people came looking for work in town.

With Marlies taking care of chores, I had leisure to be with the kids who filled me in on the latest happenings. It was fun. They had respect for my authority, not like the crotchety old patients to whom I was just a kid and quite irrelevant. Dr. Merton had been very understanding when I related to him early on that I would need to leave on short notice sometime in the near future. He had found a replacement that was willing to wait for the job until I left. Steffi had been sad to see me leave. We were like sisters of the same age who shared everything, something I knew I was going to miss very much. On the other hand, she was probably glad to have her space to herself again. Having lived with the Rheins taught me just how precious one's own four walls can be. They had been kind to me and made me feel welcome; still, I could never be totally at ease because the space I occupied did not belong to me. They had put no restrictions on me, yet I felt I had to put them on myself so as not to bother anyone. At home, I had to share a room with Hildi, and although I could not do with it whatever I liked, still, it was my room simply because my parents owed it to me.

"So, tell me guys, has Paula gone home yet, or is she still in the hospital?" I asked.

"She went home this morning," replied Hans.

"What are the babies like?"

"Wrinkly and weird looking," Matthias yelled.

"Poopy diapers," Markus sai and wrinkled his nose.

"Oh, they are so cute," Hildi cooed while Hans, with a grin, decided to abstain from voicing an opinion.

"Are you going to be their nanny?" Matthias asked.

"Yes, that's the plan," I said. "What are the twins' names?"

"Gustav and Mathilde! Can you believe it?" Hans replied with a smirk.

"Ugh, that's pretty bad."

"They named them Gustav for Father and Mathilde for Werner's mother, and you know what they'll be called? Gusti and Tilli."

"But Gusti is a girl's name," said Hildi.

"See what I mean?"

"Well, there is nothing we can do about it, is there," I said and grabbed the boys around the middle, one in each arm, and swung them round and round till they squealed and laughed. "Me too," Hildi begged.

"No, you're too big now, but come and help me unpack my bag."

We went to our room. My bed was without sheets, but otherwise nothing had changed. I had bought myself some pretty underwear and Hildi was delighted at the delicate fabric and laces. She was still wearing fleece underpants minus the mid-thigh legs that Mother cut off for summer use. Rummaging through my bag, Hildi discovered the summer dress I had bought for her. "Oh, it's so pretty. Is it for me?"

"Noo! It's mine," I said, grabbed the dress and held it against me. "See? It fits perfectly." It was a riot to watch Hildi's face change expressions as her mind worked itself from disappointment to doubt and then conviction that the dress was hers.

She tried it on right away. Hildi had grown, developed, and it was lucky for her that I had guessed her size correctly. Once she showed herself to the boys they wanted to know what I had brought for them. I pulled out a box of additional parts for the building set the little boys loved to work with. Markus was the first to grab it. "Wow!" he said. "That's great. Now we can build a trestle."

"And maybe a bridge, too, if there's enough stuff," Matthias chimed in and yanked the box out of Markus' hands. The two were still very much alike, almost the same size, hair that was chestnut brown, eyes that were gray, almost like twins. But Markus had Hans' introspective nature while Matthias, the youngest of eight, had learned early on to avoid getting hurt, physically and emotionally, by being snippy and even a little aggressive at times. Hildi, on the other hand, did not seem to belong at all; as if she didn't fit anywhere in our group of eight. She was the only one with straight blond hair and brown eyes. Father, who liked to make up nicknames for us, had often called her 'foundling,' until he discovered some unexpected consequences. Hildi had become infatuated with a young man from Father's warehouse. Not knowing anything of romantic love, and trying to come to an understanding of her feelings, she had concluded that since she was a foundling, the object of her affection must be a birth brother from whom she had become separated. That's when Father stopped calling her 'foundling.'

"Don't I get anything?" Hans asked with affected disappointment.

"Of course, you do. Here, wear it in good health," I said and dug out from my bag a wristwatch. He removed his old hand-me-down from Walter and put on the new watch. I could see it made him feel proud.

"Hey, that's great. Thanks, Fanny," he said, turning his wrist this way and that so that the watch reflected the sunshine that came in through the open windows. Seeing him that way suddenly made me realize that Hans was no longer one of 'the boys.' He had turned sixteen in April, and he had changed. His voice no longer cracked but was now a constant baritone, and his facial features were harder, squarer. Hans had become a young man. It made me feel a little shy.

"Can I have your old watch?" Markus asked and held out his hand.

"I want it," yelled Matthias and reached to grab it from Hans.

"Only one can wear it," Hans said. "And since you two are going to fight over it, I'm going to keep it for now."

"Oh, shucks," they grumbled in unison and ran off to play.

Mother came upstairs shortly after the store had closed at six pm I was hiding among the children, on purpose, because I didn't know what to expect from her. But nothing much transpired. She gave me a long, steady look, focused mainly on my head. For the first time in life I had gone to a beauty salon and had my long hair cut off. It had enough curl so that it was easy to take care of. Her eyes expressed more curiosity than anything else. Perhaps she had come to terms with the idea that I was no longer under her control. And then, quite out of the blue, I suddenly realized that I no longer felt guilty about Erna's death. I still felt bad about it, but not guilty, and certainly not the kind of guilt that had caused me to be timid and in need of punishment by totally submitting to Mother's will.

"Everything all right?" she asked.

"Doesn't Fannie look nice?" Hildi called out to Mother and pointed to my head.

"Its okay," Mother said and left. She could have said something nice about it, I thought. But compliments were not part of Mother's vocabulary.

When I went to bed that night, Hildi was still awake, or perhaps woke up from my commotion. It was hard to know, because she did have trouble sleeping at times. I remembered something I had been meaning to ask but never got around to. "Remember when you told me that you see colors around me?" I said.

"Yes."

"That's the human aura, and it shows all the emotions that people can have – bright colors mostly for good feelings, but dark ugly colors for bad stuff. I learned that from Steffi and Judith, the lady who helps her make sense of those things. And now you turn out to be psychic, too. I had a boyfriend in Venusbrunn who was psychic; he taught me a lot, too. But he died."

"Your color is changing," said Hildi. "You're sad now."

"That's right. I really liked Willi. Actually, Leon reminds me of him. They are both so nice and real sweet. Steffi used to have a lot of problems because she could see things the rest of us couldn't. And that made her feel real…"

"…bad," Hildi finished my sentence. She looked at me with her brown eyes wide open as though she was hoping and waiting for a question to be asked of her. She was fourteen years old that year but seemed so helpless and fragile.

"You, too?" I said. Hildi nodded.

And then it came; it poured out of her the way it had with Steffie at boarding school in Venusbrunn. Hildi saw fairies and gnomes, was visited by the spirits of dead people, some of which caused her to fear going to sleep. But perhaps worst of all were people she met any time, any place, whose dark auras revealed their dark characters. It was bad enough that she had difficulty learning and being called the Dummy by unfeeling classmates. Having to keep secret what she knew of the unseen side of life made things worse.

"When you mentioned my colors, you wanted to talk about it, didn't you," I said. Hildi nodded. "And then I left and you didn't have a chance. Poor Hildi," I hugged her. We talked a long time that night.

Next morning I accompanied Hildi and the boys as far as the school. It had been my school as well, a large rectangular baroque building complex that surrounded a large courtyard on all four sides. It had served many purposes over the centuries, including monastery and army barracks. Now it housed the elementary school classes one through eight. Dark and dingy was the building, and pockmarked by artillery fire from the war.

My agreement with Paula was that I should sleep at home, help her with the twins from around eight o'clock in the morning till six o'clock in the evening, and I would get my meals there as well. My pay was less than what I had received from Dr. Merton, but since I wouldn't have to pay for room and board it was acceptable to me. Paula would continue working in Werner's photo shop, which she liked very much, since I was there to take care of the babies.

Paula's mother-in-law opened the door for me when I came. Aunt Mattie, as she wanted us to call her, was a small, delicate woman with black hair and fine features. She surely hadn't passed them on to Werner who had the husky build of his father. She motioned me to be quiet. The twins had finally gone back to sleep and Paula was trying to snatch a few winks before they would be hungry again. She took me to see the babies who were lying in baskets in Paula's bedroom. They were pretty babies with quite a lot of straight dark hair and real baby faces, the type that develops its adult look only much later. While I stood there, staring at them, I got an inkling of the great responsibility that I was undertaking. But at least their mother would be close by, and if all else failed, two grandmothers were not so far away either.

I sneaked into the living room. Paula was lying on the sofa, asleep. Her face was pale; her hair had a bed-ridden look from ten days in the hospital. I picked up a magazine and read until Paula began to stir. When she looked up and saw me, she smiled. "Hey, Sis! Thank goodness you're here," she said. "Werner's mother is so helpless. You'd think she has never been around babies before."

"Well, it was only once, and that a long time ago, wasn't it," I said.

"Right," Paula admitted.

"And how is the new mother?"

"Tired, tired, tired," she said with a deep sigh. "The babies didn't sleep all night, it seems like."

"How often did you have to feed them?"

"Three times, I think."

"That much? We learned in infant classes that a baby gets fed every four hours; at six and ten in the morning, at two and six in the afternoons and again at ten o'clock at night."

"Well somebody forgot to tell my kids about it. They want to eat about every two hours. Driving me nuts." She lay back and closed her eyes. I wanted to ask a lot more questions, the kind for which I would never get an answer from Mother, because Mother never talked about what it is like to be pregnant, to give birth, and whether it hurt a lot. So secretive were people about pregnancy that women wore maternity clothes tailored to make their condition inconspicuous, and I knew of women who denied their pregnancy even when it became absurd to do so. I had to wait.

"Tell me what you want me to do," I said.

"Well, for now I just need you to help me bathe them and change diapers. Of course you can do housework as well. Werner's mother will do the cooking. She's good at that. Later, when I go back to working in the shop, you'll be alone with them all day. Do you think you can handle that?"

"Sure."

"When I feel better I want you to tell me all about Wiesenthal. Right now, I just want to sleep as much as I can. Oh, and maybe this afternoon you could help me do my hair. Meanwhile, go and see what you can help Mattie with, like washing the diapers and hanging them up. That's something we'll have to do every day."

Aunt Mattie had put on the stove a large pot of cold water with detergent and rinsed out diapers, to bring to a boil. I went shopping for groceries. Between the bakery and the butchery, I came by a stationary shop and went in to get some writing paper. Behind the counter stood a girl who looked familiar, but before I could recall her name she recognized me.

"Hey, Fannie! Fannie Sauerling, is that you?"

Her name came to me just in time. "Ulla Becker! Yep, it's me and not my shadow."

"Gosh, I haven't seen you in ages. Didn't you go to a boarding school?"

"Yes, for three years."

"When did you come back?"

"Three years ago."

"How come I never see you around? Is your Mother still so strict?"

"Hasn't changed a bit, and that's probably why you haven't seen me around."

"You'll have to fill me in some time. What are you doing now?"

"I'm nanny to my sister's twins; and you?"

"Oh yeah, I heard about your sister having twins. I work here in my Dad's shop as a sales clerk, and I do some bookkeeping, too."

"Oh yes, of course, BECKER'S STATIONARY. Do you like working for your Dad?"

"Yeah, it's okay," she said and drew it out as though she was only just now considering it.

"Not completely, huh?"

"No, not totally. How come you didn't end up in your Dad's store?"

"Oh, that's a long story. I'll fill you in sometime. I've got to get back to my sister now."

"Hey! You should come to the Army base some time. The German-American friendship Club meets on Saturdays. Any girl can go."

I had never heard of this Club, but I knew that girls who hang out with American GIs did not have the best reputation. Ulla must have read my face, because she said, "oh no, don't worry. There are chaperons and certain rules to be followed. It's all quite respectable."

"I could practice my English, I suppose," I said.

"Yeah, and you get out of the house and meet some people, huh?"

"It sounds good. Let me think about it," I said.

"Sure. Just give me a call if you want to go."

"Okay," I promised and nearly forgot what I had come for.

When I returned to Paula, her babies were awake and she was nursing the little boy while the little girl cried, and Paula looked anxiously from one to the other. I picked up the baby girl and rocked her, patted her back, talked to her, and pretty soon she became quiet, as though she was listening to my voice. The door opened and Werner came in.

"Hey, I'm glad to see you, Fanny. Paula will need all the help she can get," and with that he put his arm around my back and placing his hand on my right arm as I stood holding the baby.

"Congratulations, Werner," I said and wriggled out of his arm. In doing so, his hand loosened its grip on my upper right arm, and on its way around my back Werner snapped my bra. Cut it out, I thought, but I didn't want to say anything in Paula's presence. My hands were full of baby, so all I could do was to move out of his reach.

"Well, I have to get back to the shop," Werner said. "Just wanted to see if you were here." Then he said to Paula as he left the room, "I really need you in the shop."

Paula said to me, after he had left, "he snapped your bra, didn't he?" I nodded.

"How did you know it?"

"I recognize that sudden move; I've seen it often enough."

"Why does he do that?" I asked.

"Who knows. I guess he thinks it's funny. Here, take the baby and give me the other to feed. You can change him in the bathroom. Mother rigged up a perfect changing table for me on top of the bathtub."

One week later, Paula had gained back her strength and switched to bottle-feed the twins so that she was free to help in the shop. Werner had said he couldn't wait any longer. From then on, I took care of the twins full time. Aunt Mattie cooked the meals, which I enjoyed a great deal. As long as Werner stayed away, I was fine; when he came around, I made sure to have both hands free to keep him away from me. Because Paula was doing what she liked, working in the shop, she was usually in a good mood and enjoyed the twins.

My evenings were spent at home with the kids. Marlies got along well with Mother so that I was never bothered to do housework. Father offered me no office job, Mother made no demands on me, but I helped out whenever it became necessary. Some days I was very tired from taking care of the twins, but it was a good tired. Sometimes the kids came to see the babies. Hildi often helped me take them for a walk, and she pushed the double baby carriage with great pride. Leon promised to come in August, so that we could celebrate our birthdays together. All was well with the world.

Leon and I had planned to meet at three o'clock on Saturday afternoon by the fountain in the rear castle courtyard. It was a fairly secluded spot, enclosed on all four sides by a three story building with only one pedestrian passage to and from outside, and one passage from the rear to the front castle yard.

Mother had come to take it for granted that I would be around on weekends and evenings simply because I usually was. Aunt Mattie was able to manage the twins on Saturday mornings, and shops were closed in the afternoons.

The Saturday of Leon's visit fell on Marlies' weekend off and she went home. Hildi and I had done the usual Saturday chores: cleaning, shopping for the weekend, cooking potato soup and hot sausages for lunch, and doing dishes. Morning was done; afternoon coffee time had not yet arrived, so around two-forty-five I thought it perfectly fair to leave. Mother saw me coming from my room. She seemed puzzled, and looking me up and down in my freshly washed and starched peasant dress, white socks and immaculate white canvas sandals, she asked, "where are you going?"

"Out," I said.

"Are you going to confession?"

"No," I answered.

"Then get that dress off before it gets all wet and give the boys a bath," she said.

"Give Markus and Matthias a bath?" I said. "They're old enough to wash themselves." There must have been a hint of self-confident defiance in my voice, because Mother's eyes grew a little wider and her speech became a little more stressed as she said, "they splash too much. I want you to watch them, and wash their hair, too."

"Hildi can do it."

"Hildi has to get Walter's room ready. He's coming for the weekend."

"Well, then let Hans do it. I don't have time. I have a date."

"A date?" she snapped, as though she had never heard of such a thing. She raised her head slightly, her eyes grew big and challenging – dang it, I thought, here it comes – and with her right arm pressed tightly against her hip she said, very measured, "you can go afterward."

She did not turn away but waited for my reaction. Once again, her challenge caused me to shake inwardly, an emotional reaction my body was now producing, perhaps just from habit. I was no longer afraid of her.

"My boyfriend is waiting for me. I have no way of telling him that I'll be late." With that I maneuvered to the apartment door, and Mother maneuvered with me. Thank goodness for Father who came in at that moment, breaking up what promised to become an ugly scene.

"I'm going to meet my boyfriend," I said to him, as I slipped past him and out the door.

"Who is this boyfriend?" Father called after me. "What's his profession? Is he Catholic?"

"I'll tell you later, Dad. I'm running late."

I had no intention of introducing Leon to my parents. Father would not accept him because he was a butcher, and Mother would not accept him because he reminded her of her own societal shortcomings. Leon would be seen as nothing but a glorified handyman, while his noble, gentle character would be trod upon like pearls before swine. But, as life would have it, Father would meet Leon anyway, and much sooner than I could have anticipated.

My insides churned with excitement to such a degree that it was almost painful. Leon was already at our meeting place when I came through the shady portal into the courtyard. With a certain shyness – we hadn't seen each other since Easter - we smiled at each other, and then with tears of joy and relief I put my arms around his neck. Leon slung his arms around me and drew me close, held me quietly, not saying a word. He held me like this for a long time.

Finally, my nose nuzzling his chin and cheek, I said, "I just love your aftershave. I got a whiff of it once, in Augsburg, when I was trying to find a restroom in an apartment store. I could have sworn you stood right behind me. I actually turned to look for you. But, of course, you weren't there."

"A black day in the life of Stephanie Sauerling, huh?"

"Oh, you can't even imagine how bad it was. But you know something funny? Somehow, I always knew that things would turn out all right. I mean, I knew that I wouldn't be stuck in the street forever. Oh, how I missed you!"

"Every day I think about you, no matter what I do or where I go," he answered.

"When I'm feeding the babies I have lots of quiet time to think about you. Then I start dreaming and wishing, and then I get frustrated because I can't talk to you the way I want, or say the things I want, or hear you talking, answering me… It's bad."

"There's only one remedy for that," he said as we set out walking down through the castle's front courtyard toward the promenade.

"What's that?"

"Come to Munich."

"Oh, don't think I haven't thought about that."

"And?"

"Well, I don't know. It's like I want to, really want to, but…"

"You don't have to live in my brother's room, you know. It's rented now, anyway. But we can find you a room somewhere nearby."

"I don't know…"

"What don't you know? I'm a butcher, is that it?"

"Oh, no," I hastened to assure him.

Leon was quiet then. I could sense that something had gone wrong but wasn't sure what it was. Perhaps I hadn't convinced him that I didn't mind him being a butcher. What was so bad about being a butcher anyway. Butchers kill animals, yes, and people, including me, eat them. And father loves a good veal Schnitzel, and mother will send me not to just any butcher shop to get a good roast. Still…

We walked along in silence, not the silence of contentment that comes when two people know and understand each other so well that no words are needed. It was as if an abyss had opened up between us. How I hated this kind of silence, filled with doubt and uncertainty as to what went wrong and what words would be needed to make it right.

After a while Leon began chatting as though nothing had happened, and although I was glad for it, still, the unsaid something between us threw a shadow over our afternoon despite a rare cloudless sky and sparkling sunshine.

"I brought my motorcycle. I left it at the Brandt's butchery. We're still friends, you know. How about riding out into the hills with me tomorrow? We could stop for coffee at my home, and you could meet my mother and whoever else happens to be there."

"I'd love to. It'll be the nicest birthday I ever had," I replied, greatly relieved at the change in mood. "I'll be eighteen on Tuesday."

"Yes, and I'll be twenty-three on Friday. By this time next year I'll be a master butcher. I can teach apprentices, even open and run my own shop."

"But I still have to wait another two years before I'm of legal age."

"But if you came to Munich, you'd be on your own. Like being of legal age, huh?"

"Yeahhh…"

We had walked up the hill toward the monastery with its great view across the Hanfurt valley. We stood and watched, tried to find familiar landmarks, my house, his old work neighborhood, our parish church. Then we went into the monastery church and sat down on a bench near the front where we could see the altar clearly. It was decorated with large bouquets of flowers and countless candles. There were no people in the church; only an elderly monk, bowed from years of service, busied himself around the altar.

"You know, I could sit and think here all day," I told Leon. "It's so quiet, and peaceful here. And there are so many beautiful things to look at. Only problem is, the benches are so hard. My butt begins to hurt after a while and I have to get up."

Leon chuckled and squeeze my hand. After a while I began to feel chilly in my light summer dress and we went back outside. Leon said, "you'll never find this sort of peacefulness at home. You can only create it for yourself within your own four walls."

My own four walls. Where and how would I ever have my own four walls. I would be sharing my room with Hildi till I got married. If I had a room in Munich I would have my own four walls and I could fix them up, decorate them, use them to my taste and liking. Like building my own nest. I suddenly felt a yen to build my own nest.

"Do you think there is such a thing as a nesting instinct?" I asked.

"I should think so. How else would birds know when and how to build a nest?"

"How about people. Could we have a nesting instinct?"

"Why not," Leon replied. Then he began to hum a little tune, and when I asked him what it was, he sang,

"A bird needs a branch for to build its nest,

Fannie needs a heart whom to trust her Self."

He did not look at me but straight ahead. My eyes filled with tears again, and it really annoyed me. But I couldn't help myself because I felt overwhelmed at the realization that Leon knew me better than I knew myself.

"Come on," he said, and took my hand and pulled it into the crook of his arm. "Let's go down the other side and find a café. I know you like cake."

Around nine o'clock Leon walked me home. I had my own keys now and no longer needed to wait for the key-towel-bomb to descend on me. I would meet Leon on Sunday after morning mass at his old butchery.

I was worried about what to say to Father, should he ask me about Leon. Should I lie and describe Leon as an accomplished professional of some sort. But what kind. Actually, within a year Leon would be accomplished at a profession, the butchery profession. But nobody thought of butchery as an admirable profession. Only owners of butcher shops that were capable of producing the best sausages and most tender cuts of meat could reach a somewhat elevated status in the community. Dairy shop owners could not reach that level, neither could greengrocers, or tailors. Only sausage makers.

Father and Mother had company. Monsignor Schneider, one of our parish priests, had come for a visit, as he often did. He was a peculiar man with two doctoral degrees, one in theology and one in philosophy. His face was red as a beet and lumpy as a raspberry, the result of frostbite he had suffered during the war. He had a Western dialect and spoke a little like the French who produce the sound of words through pursing of their lips. Dr Dr. Schneider – Mother insisted on addressing both doctorates - thought his position as assistant pastor not equal to his elevated academic status. He longed for a parish of his own. In my Father, he found a willing and able contributor to whatever parish project he promoted; the war had created many needs. In my mother, he found a sympathetic ear and always a glass of really good Schnaps. In my mind's eye, I could see her glowing with pride and pleasure as she sat at the edge of her chair, ready to jump should her guest, this embodiment of wisdom and knowledge, require another Schnaps.

"Walter came home," Hildi told me. "He's in there with Mom and Dad and Dr. Schneider. Are you going to say good-night to the boys?"

"I guess so. Why do you ask?"

"Because I was supposed to put them to bed, but they don't listen to me," she said with a sigh of relief that I could take over.

"I know just what you mean," I said and went to their room. Hans was leaning over Markus' bed, trying to get him to lie down while Matthias sneaked up from behind and climbed his back. They were squealing and laughing while Hans shushed them so as not to annoy the adults in the adjacent room, but he got nowhere. Seeing me come in caused them to calm down some. "Read us a story," Matthias demanded.

"Yes, Fannie, read us a story," Markus chimed in, and even Hildi sat down on a chair with a smile of anticipation.

"All right, but you have to be real quiet, you hear?"

Hans was relieved and left the room. He was too old for fairy tales, even though some of the stories had intrigued him when he was little. It wasn't surprising that he had become interested in science fiction, which, it seemed to me, was just an extension of the fantastic fairy world. I took the big book of Grimm's Fairy tales from the table, and while I thumbed through the pages for a story that all would like, Hildi said to me, "your boyfriend must be really nice. Will you tell me about him?" I nodded.

Before I had finished the story I could hear that Dr. Schneider was leaving. Walter came in to say goodnight to the boys. They had become quiet while I was reading, had begun to doze even. But the moment they saw big brother coming through the door, they were wide awake; jumping up and down in their beds, jumping and climbing on him who was an all too willing partner in rollicking fun. Things settled down when Mother and Father came in to say goodnight. I hurried out of the room to dodge any questions Father might have. Hildi followed me to our room, and while she undressed, I told her about my date with Leon and that I would see him again on Sunday.

"I wish I had a boyfriend."

"Well, in a couple of years it'll be your turn for dancing lessons. Maybe you'll meet a nice boy then, too, just like I did."

"I already know a nice boy." She almost whispered it, while looking toward the door to make sure it was shut.

"Who is it?"

"Jordan."

"Jordan from the sales department?"

Hildi nodded. "He's so cute," she said with a blissful smile.

"Yeah, he is nice, or at least he seems that way to me." Then, a thought occurred to me, and I asked, "did you look at him with your psychic vision?"

She nodded. "His colors are real bright and pretty."

"Do you ever see people whose colors are not pretty?"

"Yes," she said and squirmed as though it was giving her physical pain to remember.

"Who?"

"I don't want to talk about it."

"Anybody I know?"

"I don't want to talk about it," she said, got into her bed and pulled the blanket over her face. After a few minutes, while I was undressing, she sat up and said to me, "I can't sleep now. Tell me a story, a nice one?"

I guessed that some bad image was giving her trouble. I laid down beside her and painted for her a verbal picture of lying in a beautiful meadow with lots of flowers and a gentle breeze wafting through the swaying grasses, this way and that, so gentle, rousing the scent of earth and flowers, and carrying the gnit-gnats of insects, and the song of birds spilling over the meadow. And Hildi was asleep.

I met Leon after the nine-thirty mass. I sent the kids home with the message that I would be spending the day with Leon. Along the way, the thought of Mother and what she might expect of me or have planned for me came to mind and made me feel uneasy. Perhaps I should have told her that I would not be around to cook dinner. Then again, she could have asked me if I would be. But it would never occur to Mother to ask me what I want.

The weather was glorious; the sky was blue, not a cloud anywhere in sight, which was a rare thing indeed. I wore my blue Dirndl dress again, white socks and my canvas sandals that I had given the once over with the whitening liquid. I was looking forward to a ride on Leon's motorcycle.

He was waiting in the street by his cycle. "I should have told you to bring a sweater or something," he said, when he noticed that I had none. "It can get pretty drafty. I'll find something," and with that he went back into the house and came out with a light, colorless jacket that belonged to the butcher's wife. I put it on but I didn't like that it spoiled the look of my immaculate outfit.

"Trust me," Leon said with a smile, as his eyes followed mine, drifting from the jacket to my dress and back. "You'll be glad you have it." He wore an old corduroy jacket that belonged to his butcher friend. Then he placed a couple of clasps on his pant legs to keep them from getting caught up in any rotating cycle parts. Cap and goggles came next, and then he climbed onto the motorcycle. With a grand hand gesture he invited me to get behind him. It took a little time for me to arrange my skirt in such a way that it wouldn't fly over my head, find my footholds without getting grease on my white sandals, put my arms around Leon and try to feel safe and secure behind him. "Always lean into the curve," he told me. Then he started the motor, revved it a couple of times, and off we went.

It took me a while to begin feeling secure on this two-wheeling machine. Eventually, my grip around Leon's middle loosened a bit and I figured out how to see the countryside despite the blurring wind. A glorious patchwork of woods and meadows, fields and streams, hills and valleys made this country the precious jewel to which we city dwellers turned in every season and for any and all occasions.

We planned to visit his family at dinnertime. Meanwhile we just rode around and I was very glad to have the jacket. There was very little traffic; most country lovers were still in the city, coming home from church and preparing Sunday dinner.

"Have you ever been to the border," Leon asked, as we leaned into one of the many curves on this very windy road through hills and villages and around farms. The words blew by me on the wind; I could just make out the word border.

"No, never," I shouted into his ear.

I was beginning to get chilled on my bare legs and was glad when Leon stopped. We had passed a few signs that announced the approach to the Russian occupied zone. We got off the cycle and looked around.

"So, where's the border," I asked.

"Right here. See the barbed wire?"

"That's it? This is where the Russian sector begins? But I can step right over this wire."

"But don't do it," replied Leon.

"But, anywhere else I can walk from the American sector into the British sector, but we're not supposed to walk into the Russian sector? Who says so?"

"Look, there come the border guards."

Indeed, three uniformed young men with guns shouldered came walking along the plowed strip of land beyond the barbed wire. They walked past, then disappeared from sight as trees on the Western side blocked our view. After a little while they reappeared.

"These are Russians?" I asked

"No, they're East Germans."

"So why are they patrolling this border?"

"Because they're under the domination of Russia. And it's very clever too. Germans won't mind Germans patrolling the border nearly as much as if the guards were Russians.

"But why all this barbed wire?"

"There is a suspicion that Russia wants to make this border permanent."

"So, all along this border, no one is allowed to cross?"

"Not from West to East – not that anyone would want to - and not from East to West. And they will shoot to kill over there if someone tries to escape."

"So it's really a prison. How strange, to think that all of East Germany is a prison. This border goes right through the Rhoen. My Father had customers over there, and he knows a lot of people. And the parents of those guards might have been friends with him. And people who have family on both sides are now cut off from each other. And now we're enemies, even deadly enemies."

"Sad, isn't it."

It took a while for all this to sink in and for me to digest it. The appearance of this so-called border was innocent enough. It was simply a roll of barbed wire, nothing else. And one could step over it easily enough. We strolled along the border toward North, then turned and strolled along it going South. The guards were always in sight. Suddenly, I saw a rare carline thistle on the East side of the border just beyond the wire roll. Short and squat, it clung close to the ground, and its slender silvery blossom pedals glistened in the sun.

"Leon, look! See the Silver thistle?" I said and pointed.

"Yes," he said absentmindedly while watching the border guards. They didn't seem to pay any attention to us. They had their backs turned toward us and mumbled among themselves.

"I'm going to get it," I said.

"Are you crazy!" Leon nearly yelled it. It took me by surprise to see him so riled up.

"But it's good luck to find a Silver thistle," I said. "Maybe these guys could get it for me." And before thinking it through, I called to them.

"Don't do anything stupid," Leon pleaded. The guards ignored us. I called again.

"Shhhh, don't talk to them," Leon implored.

"Why not," I argued. "Are they going to shoot us if we talk to them?"

"You never know. In Berlin they shoot people trying to cross the border."

"Well, this is not Berlin."

It seemed to me that Leon was awfully fearful. "Hey! Grenzer!" I called to the guards. "There's a Silver thistle growing over there. Would you please pick it for me?"

They whispered among themselves, then one of them came a little closer and said, "you can come and get it yourself."

Had I taken time to study the expression on his face I might have changed my mind. Instead, before Leon had a chance to hold me back, I stepped over the wire and walked right over to the flower. "Don't be stupid!" I heard coming from Leon, as I bent down to pick it. I heard a sound like a wail behind me. When I stood up, I felt a hard object in my back. I turned to look and found myself staring down the barrel of a gun.

"Oh, you scared me," I said reproachfully, trying to push the menacing object aside. Instead, the other two guards now also pointed their guns at me.

"Don't you know these plants are under nature protection?" the first guard said slowly and menacingly. There was nothing friendly in his face. His cold, hard stare began to disturb me. Still, this had to be just a big joke. I was told to come and get it, and I did.

"Alright, get going," said the first guard with a harsh voice, his head pointing in the northerly direction.

"You mean..." I looked to Leon. He seemed to be in awful agitation, stepping from one leg to the other, looking back and gesticulating as if to get someone's attention. His face was contorted in utter alarm.

"Leon!" I yelled while the guns pushed me forward.

"What are you doing?" he shouted. "Grenzer! Let her go. She didn't do anything. You told her to come and get the flower herself. Why are you doing this?"

"Shut up!" one of guards yelled back.

"I'm going to notify the authorities!" Leon shouted after us.

"Yeah, you do that," one of the guards shouted back and let out a derisive laugh. It began to dawn on me that I might be in more danger than I could have imagined. Fear began to grip my inside.

"Stephanie!" Leon called after me, anguished, frustrated, and fearful. "Don't you worry. I'll call your parents!"

"No! Don't do that!" I yelled back as I whipped around in near panic. Leon stood there, motionless, with a baffled look on his face. The gun in my back persuaded me to move forward. A mock border authority in my head declared that we were now in the Russian occupied zone of East Germany.

Once inside East Germany, one of the guards walked ahead with his gun shouldered. The other two followed behind me, their guns still at the ready. I was marched down a path that followed along the barbed wire for perhaps a mile or so. To the left of the path lay the wide strip of plowed land that was meant to reveal escapee footprints. After a while, the path veered off toward a wooded area. The ground was muddy from the last rain and forced me to watch my steps carefully. Still, I slipped and slid around, and pretty soon my immaculate white sandals and socks looked like splotchy brown shoes. The guards were walking fast; they wore boots nearly up to their knees. Handsome, slender guys in green uniforms, belted around the waist, and a snappy little garrison cap on their heads, they were nice to look at. Surely, they had girl friends and mothers and fathers. They hadn't fallen from the sky or were grown out of cabbage heads. So how could they shoot unarmed countrymen, I wondered.

I had trouble keeping up with them. Whenever I slowed down, the guard who walked directly behind me poked at my back with his gun. To my question where they were taking me they answered with silence. Somewhere along my forced march in the forbidden zone I dropped the unlucky Silver thistle in a mossy spot.

A jumble of thoughts and feelings that occupied my mind began to make me feel rather queer. On the one hand, I was, perhaps, the only person who ever accomplished this unconventional border crossing into East Germany That gave me a real kick. On the other hand, Leon was left holding the bag, so to speak. Our birthday celebration was doomed once again, and I hated to think of the problems I had caused him. He would meet my parents; he would tell them what had happened to me. Father would learn that Leon was a butcher – oh drat!

We came to the wooded area and walked through it. Coming out on the other side we saw the remains of what had once been a farming village. The inhabitants, of course, had all been moved out. It was that way all along the entire eight hundred and seventy mile border. Some parts of the village had been turned into barracks for the border guards and their vehicles. My three guardians marched me to the largest of the buildings, and when we entered, I felt scared. For the first time, it dawned on me that I might end up in a jail, or prison, or perhaps a kind of holding pen. There I would remain until my parents worked out something with the appropriate authority, which would then work out something with a higher authority in the West, who would then work out something with a higher authority in the East, who would then work out something with the local border guards. In the meantime, I could be sitting behind bars for days, or weeks, or months, or – heaven forbid – even longer. And I had no change of clothes!

A door was flung open by a guard who shouted something into the room, and then I was pushed inside. It was a dank, dark room with few furnishings. Behind a huge desk sat an officer who was busy writing something. My three guards saluted, then stood back and waited. When the officer looked up and saw me, the guard whom the others called Klaus said, "we caught her sneaking across the border."

"That's not true! You told me to come and get the flower myself," I complained.

"Is it your habit to obey orders from East German border guards?" the officer asked, his face straight and stern. I could see the irony in what had happened and couldn't help but grin.

"You won't think it so funny when you stand trial for espionage," he said. It very deftly derailed my attempt at nonchalance. That's when the brutality of the Russian occupation really sank in: they were using Germans, just like me, to prevent other Germans from leaving the East, from going anywhere they pleased. They used German guards to shoot and kill other Germans who were determined to try anyway.

I had no time to contemplate this awful fact any longer; the officer began to question me. He wanted to know if my parents had put me up to this stunt, who they were, their political affiliation, and their profession. It went on for hours. Dinnertime was long past and I became very hungry. My request for something to eat was ignored. My need for a toilet was heeded. I was taken to the nearest out-house, a stinky run-down shack, with nothing but coarse cut-up newspaper for sanitary use.

Once back in the old farmhouse, I was told to wait in a small room that had no furniture other than two chairs and a table. The walls were still papered, although torn and smudged in places There were brighter, cleaner rectangular areas where pictures had once been hanging. It had surely been someone's bedroom at one time, and it seemed to breath sadness for having been abandoned. A sense of loss and sadness came over me, sadness and loss at being forced to leave one's home, the abode of many generations, who had made their living off the land. They had lived in harmony with nature, had cared for livestock and fields, had known how to honor the seasons and revel in that which nature provided. Now, they probably existed in some cramped apartment, in some huge tenement building, in some gigantic and polluted city, far away, torn from their roots, and without hope of ever returning. I felt for them.

The windows of this room were nailed shut and the panes were painted over. I could hear vehicles coming and going, telephones ringing, mumbling from people I couldn't see. When I tried to open the door, I discovered that it was locked. My stomach rumbled like crazy, and I wished that Leon would come and rescue me.

Leon. I recalled the peculiar look on his face when I yelled "no" to him. I could see now that it was a dumb thing to say. Of course he had to let my parents know what had happened. He had looked so sad, or unsure. I couldn't quite define that expression. I had never seen it on him before. Saturday came to mind, when I had also said "no" to a meeting with my parents. He had become very quiet then, and I had felt a great abyss open between us. How I hated that feeling.

Eventually, it was getting quiet outside as it grew dark. A weird sensation of having been forgotten by the world came over me. The twilight zone must be like that, I thought. There was nothing for me to do but prepare myself for the night. I pushed together the two chairs, seats facing, and tried to lie down on the combined platform. But the seats were molded to fit behinds, and the chair backs had too many cross pieces to allow my legs through; it was no good. Forgotten by the world, ignored by authorities, left hungry and thirsty, and now not even a bed for the night. It was too much. I cried.

With my arms crossed on the table and my head on my arms, I remembered the night when I was stranded in Augsburg. Somehow, I had known deep down inside that I would be all right. Now, here in East Germany, the memory of that sensation and the fact that it was proved right kept my fears in check. I dozed off.

I didn't know what time it was when someone came to the door and opened it. Three guards I hadn't seen before came in and told me to get up; they would take me back. I breathed a sigh of relief. We climbed into a vehicle that resembled an American Jeep and started off into the pitch black. It was so dark that I couldn't see beyond the headlights of the vehicle. To my question where they would take me, I received no answer. I had no clue in which direction we were going. It was cold and drafty in that vehicle. After a short drive, they stopped and told me to get out.

"Are you letting me go?" I asked half glad, half panicky.

"Yes."

"Is this West Germany? Which way should I go?"

"Anyway you like," one of them said and laughed. "But if you come back our way you'll be in real trouble."

I figured that continuing in the direction I had been driven might be the right way. In the shine of the headlights I began to walk ahead. The ground felt fairly solid and even.

There was no moon that night, and once the Jeep turned back I saw nothing.

When my eyes had adjusted to the dark I began to feel my way forward, hands stretched out in front of me to guard against trees and shrubs. All the fairy characters of my childhood would have haunted me that night if I had had a mind for them. But all my senses strained to make out the terrain before me. I feared falling into a creek, or getting shredded by a barbed wire fence, or trampled by a dairy bull. I stumbled around for probably an hour before I saw a faint light in the distance. I aimed for it and eventually arrived at a farmhouse. The light came from a tall post in the middle of the farmyard. A dog began barking furiously in his kennel, and pretty soon a door opened and voices called out into the night.

I was so glad to see and hear people, West German people, that I nearly cried with relief. The farmer stood in the door, waving a flashlight around. On seeing me, he yelled, "what on earth are you doing out there in the middle of the night?" His wife showed up behind him and called out, "dear God! You look a mess. Come inside."

I hadn't notices just how cold it had gotten during my odyssey. My clothes were wet from the night's dew and my legs and the skirt of my dress were filthy from mud splashes. I was shivering. The farmer's wife brought a blanket and wrapped it around me. Then I told them my weird story

Home, family, and the extended family of Father's employees, some of whom had been with us since before Father married Mother, buzzed like a beehive. Everyone wanted to know what had happened, how it happened, why it happened. Some had thought they would never see me again. Mother blamed me for upsetting Father's weekend. Father had called the police for help and was embarrassed about it. The newspaper called to do an interview, the West German boarder guards wanted to know what I had seen and heard in the East. But the one person from whom I wanted to hear most was silent.

Leon had gone to see my parents and tell them what had happened. When he was told there was nothing further for him to do, he left. To Munich? To his family home? I didn't know. For the second time, unforeseen events had ruined our birthday plans. Perhaps we weren't meant to be together

"I saw your boyfriend when he was here," Hildi said with a big smile.

"Did you see him while he talked to Father?" Hildi nodded. "Did Father ask him anything personal, like where he works?"

"I don't remember him asking, but Leon mentioned that he works at Brandt's butchery."

"Oh, drat!"

"Why? What's wrong?"

"I didn't want Father to know."

"Leon looked awfully sad. Are you going to write to him and tell him that he doesn't have to worry about you anymore, that you're okay?"

"He called me crazy, and stupid! Let him write first."

It didn't take long for life's routines to take over. On one of my errands for Paula, I came by the stationary shop again. Thinking that I might nurture a friendship with Ulla, I went in to talk with her. When she invited me to the German-American Friendship Club again, I agreed.

"You can practice your English, dance, and have a good time," she said. "It's every Saturday afternoon, from two to five o'clock. If you come here, say about two, we could walk together. It's more fun that way. Just ring the bell by the house door, not the shop door."

"I know. You live upstairs. I'll see you around two? I expect it'll take a good half hour to get to the base."

"That's right. Don't forget your ID, you'll need it to get in. And wear something pretty."

"Don't I always?" I said with a frown, and we both laughed because we both knew how old-fashioned my mother used to dress us.

At two o'clock the following Saturday, I showed up at her front door and rang the bell. She was downstairs in a jiffy. Looking me over, she exclaimed, "oh, that's so cute." I was wearing my new red-and-white striped dress, with the stripes going vertically except at the hem of the flared skirt where a broad band of stripes went horizontally. But the best part was the fitted bodice that had a V-neck in front and back. At the shoulders, the front and back came together in narrow strips that tied together in a knot.

"You can wear that, you're so thin," she said with a bit of envy. "I would need a brassiere and it would show." Ulla wore a flared skirt with large white flowers on a black background and a dainty white blouse with white embroidery down the front. She had always worn her hair short and stylish. During the previous year she had spent some time in a British household to learn English. It was an exchange program, much like the German-American friendship Club. They were designed to foster friendly relations among the European nations, which had only very recently emerged from a most devastating war.

I was not used to compliments and felt a bit weird about getting one from Ulla. But soon I felt at ease, a state of being that seemed to come naturally to Ulla, and we caught up on some of the years that we had spent in different schools. Before we knew it, we had arrived at the US Army base, which was located near the outskirts of Hanfurt in the West. We came to the guards who checked our IDs, and upon mentioning the Club they allowed us to pass. Ulla led the way and I followed. We came to a building that seemed to have been created for social events rather than dorms for the GIs. Some girls had already arrived, among them Ingrid, whose younger sister had been in my class.

The club was a hall with large windows facing south. It had a bright, friendly feel about it. Couches and chairs were arranged in convenient conversation groups, and a jukebox provided the music. An impressive looking lady of perhaps forty was seated on one of the couches. Ulla headed straight for her and introduced me to the lady who was the chaperone. Her name was as plain as her appearance was remarkable – Mueller. She had coal-black hair combed back out of her face and tied in a large knot on the back of her head. Her complexion was smooth, she wore make-up and nailpolish and gypsy-style golden hoop earrings Her blue silk dress was simple and elegant with short sleeves, adorned only by a décolletage that showed off her well shaped bosom. A silky fringed shawl wrap that glittered in the most exquisite shades of blue and green completed her outfit.

For a while, I could hardly take my eyes off her. What a difference from Mother and her lackluster everything. Frau Mueller greeted me with a handshake, and then asked me to sit by her side so that she might inform me of the rules of the Club. The emphasis lay on fostering friendly relations with the US soldiers. The first and most important rule was that there would be no dating the soldiers we would meet at the club, and therefore, no leaving the premises with any of them. All interactions were to be polite and casual and drinks were non-alcoholic. Frau Mueller stressed what we had learned in dancing school as part of social etiquette: that we were not to turn down any soldier who wanted to dance with us. We could, of course, sit out a dance to take a break, but we could not deny a dance to one soldier because we didn't like his looks, and then turn around and dance with another one. That way, no one would be offended.

Quite a few soldiers were standing or sitting around. Ulla and I sat together and it didn't take long for her to be asked to dance. I was curious to find out just how much or how little my school English would be useful. The sounds of American English had always intrigued me. They seemed to originate in the center of the mouth where tongue action would roll and wad them into syllables before letting them come out through the lips.

When Ulla's dancer brought her back, he asked me to dance next. He was a short little guy, with dark hair and dark impish eyes. He was dressed in a clean uniform while some of the other guys wore civilian clothes. He said he was from Texas, had a large family, and loved to dance. He was quite good. I didn't have to try my English much because he did all the talking, of which I understood very little. And it didn't matter anyway, because I was thinking of Leon and how we had danced together and how happy I had been. I ached inside.

When the music had finished, the little GI asked if I would like something to drink. Yes, I would like some apple juice, I said. He went and brought me a small bottle of juice and then returned to his comrades.

Ulla had a drink also, and while we sipped on our juices, Ingrid came over. We had been in the same elementary school, even if not in the same grade. She filled me in on her younger sister, Renate, who attended a teacher training college because she planned to be a governess. She was one year older than I. During the year following the end of the war, all children were grouped together according to educational need, not age. Suddenly, Ingrid said, "didn't I read something about you in the paper recently? Something to do with the border guards? What was that?"

"Oh, it became a big stink, that's what. I saw a silver thistle beyond the West's borderline and asked the East Zone Grenzer to get it for me. He said to come and get it myself, and I did. So they grabbed me and took me to their station. Then they had a lot of questions, and later that night, when it was pitch black, they took me back across and simply dumped me somewhere, in the middle of nowhere."

"And that's all?"

"Yeah, that's all."

"Weren't you scared?" Ingrid asked.

"Not at first. But later, oh yes; when I felt the gun in my back, I got real scared."

"They threatened you with a gun?" Ingrid said in disbelief.

"Oh yes, they did."

The music started up again and some GIs headed in our direction. The little Texan came for Ulla, a tall handsome guy in civilian clothes, that were unmistakably American fashion, came for Ingrid, and another GI in uniform came for me. His name was Joe, GI Joe he said, but I didn't know what to make of that. He was not a good dancer, and I was glad when the music ended. When Ingrid came around again, I asked her about her sister's education. It turned out that she first had to complete an apprenticeship either as cook, seamstress, or ironing person. She had chosen cook, before entering the school in Hamburg, where she was now. I counted backward and discovered that I could have also completed an apprenticeship by now if I had begun right after finishing the business school of Venusbrunn. Oh, drat!

"Renate had known for a long time that she wanted to be a governess. So she went right to it after eighth grade," said Ingrid.

"What are you doing?" I asked.

"I work at the Dresdner Bank."

"Do you like it?"

"Yes, I do. You meet so many people, and important people, too. Your Dad's company has an account there, you know?"

No, I didn't know. How could I, having been stuck in the kitchen as mother and housekeeper, I wanted to tell her. But having learned about Renate's good fortune made me feel so jealous, that I wanted to cry about my own wasted years of misery. I clammed up.

Ulla and I left promptly at five o'clock. In answer to her question, I told her that I had liked it at the Club and would come again.

"By the way," she said. "I've been meaning to ask you: when you got kidnapped by the border guards, were you alone or was someone with you?"

"Leon was with me. We had driven there on his motorcycle."

"Who is Leon?"

"I guess you could call him my boyfriend. I met him in dancing school."

"Can I meet him some time?"

"He lives in Munich now. I don't know if I'll see him again. After that border thing he went to tell my parents what happened. Then he left and I haven't heard from him since."

"Too bad."

"Do you have a boyfriend?" I asked.

"Not really. I know a bunch of guys, but none of them could be called a boyfriend. My Dad is worried sick that I'll bring home a GI for a son-in-law one of these days. There's no danger of that, though. I haven't met any that I would be interested in other than just dancing, and keeping up my English. It's so different from British English that I have a hard time with it."

We had reached her home, said good-bye and she went inside. In another five minutes, I was at my house. Lucky Renate was foremost in my mind, so when I reached the second floor where Father's office was located, with a certain attitude of daring, I went inside. As luck would have it, he was just about to leave the office and go upstairs.

"Dad, I need to talk to you for a minute." Apparently, there was enough resolve in my voice that Father stopped and listened. "I want to be a governess. I found out today that I need to do an apprenticeship as cook or seamstress, and then I can enter the teacher training institute for two years."

"You want to be a governess? I never knew anything about that."

"Well, maybe its because you never asked me."

"But you can work here in the office. That's why you went to Venusbrunn, to learn business courses."

"I wanted to go there, yes, but I had no idea what I would learn there. And you never told me. Do you know why I wanted to go there?"

"Because Erna had gone there before you."

"No Dad. I wanted to go there because I had read a book about a girl in boarding school, and all the fun she had. That's why. I thought I would have a lot of fun there, too."

Father sat down with a long face. "But you can still work here in the office. Miss Schulz is leaving soon, and then you can take her place. It's a profession. It's an income."

"Typing invoices all day? No, thanks, Dad."

"I could probably find something else for you."

"No Dad. You didn't have a job when I wanted one, and now I don't want one anymore. I want to be a governess."

"I'll have to talk to your Mother about that," he said and headed out the door. I followed him upstairs. Father opened the front door and went inside, I followed him. Mother came from the kitchen and asked me where I had been. In her face brewed storm clouds, the little boys were running around playing catch, Hildi tried to quiet them but could not, Hans was leaning against a wall with his face in a book.

"I was with Ulla Becker," I said.

"How dare you just leave without telling anyone where you're going," she said, harshly. Father went to the living room to watch television.

"Alright, next time I'll tell you. You might as well know right now that from now on, Saturday afternoons belong to me alone."

"I don't believe I'm hearing right," Mother said in her slower, threatening voice and reached for a clothes hanger from the hall stand. With two quick steps I was at the bathroom door but it was locked. I had no choice but to face Mother, so I said firmly, "Mother, I work all day and then I come home and work some more. I need to have time off, and Saturday afternoons are it."

She looked at me for a moment, then, to my surprise, she put the clothes hanger back, and just ordered me to fix supper for the children.

I went dancing at the German-American Club every Saturday, with or without Ulla, and enjoyed it very much. At other times, Ulla, Ingrid and I got together at the Italian ice cream parlor, or went to a neighborhood dance, or to the movies. Mother didn't say much anymore. Marlies, the maid, didn't run away like those before her had done. Hildi was old enough now to look after the boys, and take care of chores that I used to do. I felt very much in control of my life and it gave me a great deal of confidence.

The soldiers at the club were very nice and polite. One in particular, Patrick by name, was a great dancer and he often danced with me, but he also danced with other girls because it was expected. When he danced with me I'd half close my eyes, pretend he was Leon who held me close and protectively. Taking a deep breath of his after-shave lotion, which was the same as Leon's, I'd be happy for a little while. But each dance ended with a letdown, because it was not Leon that I had danced with, and I ached for his touch and embrace. I had not heard from him, and I had not written.

I came to know some of the soldiers who were regulars at the club, and there were always new faces. Frau Mueller ruled the club like a regal mother hen, who helped me with interpretation if Ulla was not present. I became acquainted with a few of the regular girls, and there, too, were often new faces. But now and again, one of the regular GIs stopped coming, and I wondered why. When I mentioned it to Ulla, she giggled.

"What?" I asked.

"Well think about it. A certain GI comes every Saturday and sees and dances with the same girl every Saturday, and then neither he nor the girl show up anymore?"

"Oh, I get it. They're seeing each other outside the club. But we're not supposed to do that, right?"

"Well, who's going to stop it? They can't control when two people fall in love. And as long as they don't come to the club anymore, who cares. I'll tell you a little secret: One of the guys has his eyes on me. I like him too, and I'm tempted…"

"What's stopping you?"

"I like to dance, and this club is the only regular dance hall I know of."

"Oh what problems you have!" I said and laughed. "I wish they were mine."

Paula's twins thrived. Like Mother, Paula was happy to be working in the store, and her mother-in-law prepared tasty meals. Father had wanted my income to save it for me, with a totally inadequate allowance held back for me. Once again, it had taken all my nerve to persuade him to let me keep it. I needed to learn to handle money, I had said, and he did not argue with it. But first I had to buy some pretty new clothes.

On leaving Paula's house one day through a hallway that separates the living area from the shop, her husband, Werner, came out of the shop. I said good-bye as I headed for the house door, but quickly, Werner came behind me and placed his hand against the door to keep it shut. I was trapped between him and the door.

"What are you doing?" I demanded.

"What's the big hurry?" he asked.

I moved away from him and said, "no hurry, just ready to leave."

"I hear you spend a lot of time at the Army base."

"I go dancing there."

"With Ulla Becker."

"What's it to you?"

"I know things about Ulla," he said slowly, with emphasis on "know."

"Well, it's a small town. She probably knows things about you, too."

"I think you have a boyfriend," he said, and he moved closer.

"Get away from me," I growled and reached for the door. Werner stepped back and laughed. Whatever respect I had for him as a human being, professional, brother-in-law, and father evaporated instantly by way of his repulsive laughter. It seemed to come from some ugly inner recess that not even he might have been aware of. Once out on the street I shook with disgust. It was deplorable to think that this man was the father of beautiful twins, husband to my sister, and, therefore, related to me. And what about Paula. How could I spend all day in her home and not let on that I had seen a very ugly side of her husband.

"Did you write to Leon?" Hildi asked me one day, out of the blue.

"Why do you ask?"

"Because you don't look very happy," she answered.

"No, I'm not happy," I admitted.
"So why don't you write?"
"I should, I know…"

"But?" Hildi could be so wise.

"I don't really know. I want to, and then I don't want to. I can't forget that he called me stupid and crazy. I mean, I get enough name-calling from Mother."

Of course I really had acted stupid and crazy at the border – well, perhaps not stupid but definitely too quick and without thinking the matter through. But, I figured, that was for me to do if I wanted, but not for him to call me on. And now that he hadn't written, I didn't even know if he still cared for me. It was a painful thought, but going dancing at the army base helped to soothe it.

November came and with it a lot of rain. I had forgotten my umbrella one day and, out and about on errands, I stepped into Becker's shop to wait out the rain. Ulla was not busy and we started chatting. She told me that she had begun dating the GI she had mentioned to me. She swore me to secrecy because she still wanted to go dancing at the base.

"Werner told me one day that he knows things about you. What do you think he meant? What does he know?"

"Werner, your brother-in-law? I have no idea. He probably thinks because I know a lot of guys that I sleep with them. Maybe that's what he does, stepping out on your sister, so he thinks other people do the same. But I don't. I can't help that a lot of guys like me. I don't even know why; I mean, I'm not exactly gorgeous." Ulla was right. There were girls who were much prettier than she. And she wasn't especially statuesque either, or had gorgeous legs. But she had a voluptuous laugh, a sexy laugh. Like a voluptuous body, it seemed to tantalize the opposite sex with an imagined promise of sexual pleasures.

"He came on to me one day, can you imagine?"

"You see? Just as I thought. I heard things about him," she said and laughed at the irony. "Then again, who knows if there's anything to it. Hanfurt is a nest, and you saw for yourself what the gossip mills can do. And really, I never slept with any of the guys that I know. I wouldn't dare. It's a mortal sin, and I'd go straight to hell."

That's what we were taught. But I didn't believe it, hadn't for some time. I could not accept that a good person who made one mistake and then died in a car crash before he could go to confession would go straight to hell. But I didn't want Ulla to think I encouraged her to do what she knew to be wrong.

"Roger does want to have sex, though," she continued, "but I won't. Oh, he's such a good dancer, and a good kisser – I hope he doesn't dump me because I won't have sex with him." I met her boyfriend, Roger, on the following Saturday at

122

the club. He was a good-looking guy, quite tall, with dark straight hair, dark slightly bulging eyes, and a cute nose that was a stark contrast to his square face. There was a certain sense of aloofness about him, as though he was taller than everyone else and was used to looking above other people's heads. Or perhaps he was looking around, a searching that had become habit. When Ulla introduced me to him he had a chance to show off his fairly good German. He had learned it at home from his German grandparents, he said, and they would like nothing better than to have him bring home a German bride. Roger had his arm around Ulla's shoulder and smiled at her when he said it; she blushed at this revelation. Then they danced, and Roger danced with me, and I watched him dance with others; he was always polite and seemed to show great interest in each of his dance partners. Ulla danced with other GIs to keep their secret safe, and I thought it just great that Roger didn't seem a bit jealous and never checked up on her.

The last Sunday of November turned out to be the first Advent Sunday that year. Mother had bought the traditional advent wreath made from spruce branches. Hildi went to the attic to get the candle holders, then she and the boys went shopping for groceries and red candles, while I took the large sheet cake to the bakery and Hans went to the milk shop to buy five liters of milk with two milk cans. I did not go dancing at the base that day.

Christmas would be much more fun this year, I figured, because we would have babies around. The twins were almost six months old now, old enough to look with wide eyes and wonder at a beautiful Christmas tree. Mother would be happy and sing blissfully off key. Walter would be at home. He and Hans always came up with the funniest gags. Hildi had joined the choir, and we would sing the midnight mass from the gallery. Markus and Matthias, who had turned ten and nine in early November, would not have to fight over who got to hold the babies because there was one for each. Paula and Werner would, of course, celebrate with us; Werner's widowed mother would come along. Sometimes it seemed to me that Paula spent so much time at our house because she could always count on someone being around who would take the twins off her hands. Then again, maybe the reason was that Werner was on his best behavior at our house.

I didn't go dancing during the four weeks of Advent, that time for inner preparation for the celebration of the birth of Christ. But I missed going to the club. I missed the chance to imagine being in Leon's arms, missed the attention and compliments I received from the GIs, missed moving in rhythm to beautiful music. I went to see a movie with Ulla one Sunday afternoon. She and Roger had become inseparable, she told me. She no longer went to the base; instead, Roger spent a lot of time at her home where her parents and brother and sister enjoyed his company very much.

"I thought your father was worried that you might fall for a GI," I mentioned.

"I'm sure he does worry, but he doesn't let on. Anyway, there's nothing he can do about it and he knows it. My Dad likes to drink, and whenever Roger is over, we usually end up drinking quite a bit. Then things get really lively, because my Dad knows a lot of jokes. He likes those get-togethers. Besides, you know how people like Americans. They seem so sophisticated, you know? So attractive in their snappy uniforms. And their dollars buy so much."

"I know. I've seen it in our store when a soldier or an army wife comes to buy something, and they call me to interpret. It makes me sick, though, when I see a German fawn over an American."

I had never told Father that I went dancing at the US army base. Father did not like Americans. He blamed Eisenhower for letting the Russians have the largest piece of German soil to occupy, something they were determined to keep and make into a separate country from the West. He detested chewing gum, make-up, bad manners, and the wasteful use of electricity in the army barracks, payment for which Germans were responsible. But the one thing that had turned him against Americans the most was his four-week stint in the local jail. It was the result of a house search, conducted by American and German authorities who suspected black-market activities. Adding insult to injury: Father, member of the local merchant gentry, was made to sweep the streets in front of the jail, in painful and humiliating sight of Hanfurt citizens.

"You should come over some time, you'll see, we have a lot of fun," Ulla said.

"I'd like that, maybe after Christmas."

"On New Year's Eve," said Ulla quickly. "That's the perfect day for a party. We're going to have a sweep-out-the-old-year party. Roger will come, too. He should be able to get leave, and he can even spend the night here if he needs to. And, noo, we're not going to have sex," she added in answer to my raised eyebrows. "No, I told you, and I told him. But honestly, he's bugging me an awful lot. I just hope I can hold out."

"Hold out for what?"

"I don't know. Just hold out. Not have sex."

"In other words, you won't have sex with him, period."

"Right."

"Does Roger know that? I mean, does he understand and believe that you will never ever have sex with him?"

"Of course. I told him so."

"Or does he think sooner or later he'll wear you down?"

In Ulla's face, resolve and despair created a most hilarious expression as she said, "that's what worries me. Don't laugh."

"Oh, I'm sorry," I said, trying to keep a straight face. "But really, I wish you could have seen your face."

Ulla smiled. "Well, there's nothing to do but wait and see," she said.

Paula was frantic when I got to her house on Monday morning. Her Mother-in-law had come down with the flu, and Paula needed to look after her and cook as well, but the twins kept her from it. I sat down on the floor with them, on a blanket, near Paula's very pretty Christmas tree that had white candles, colorful ornaments and lots of heavy tinsel that hung straight as icicles. Taffy and Tilli, as I called them, were good babies. I couldn't bring myself to think of them as Gustav and

125

Mathilde. They ate well, were usually happy, and had slept through the night since they were three months old.

As I sat there and watched them looking at the tree and cooing and reaching for it, it suddenly occurred to me that I was like a surrogate mother to them. I was with them eight hours a day, five days a week. That was almost more than Paula spent with them. How long did I want to keep doing this nanny job, I wondered. I liked it, yes, but there were lots of other things I liked also: art and music, and being a governess. Father thought of my business training as a career, yet he had never seen fit to have me complete an apprenticeship, like everyone else's daughter was doing. I had discovered that without a successfully completed apprenticeship, I would not have a profession. I would just be a laborer with a smaller income than otherwise. For Walter, his heir apparent, he considered it important. Not so for us girls though. We would get married and didn't need a career, he figured. But what if I never found a husband, or just didn't want to get married. And that one of his daughters might end up widowed or even divorced, and in need of earning a living, I'm sure never entered Father's mind. How very shortsighted. Black clouds were already gathering over Paula's marriage.

It became clear to me that I needed to talk to somebody about my future. I had no idea who it could be, but I would ask questions. I was good at it. And it was pretty certain that I would get nowhere while waiting for Father to make a move.

Sylvester evening at home, Paula and Werner came early, only too glad to have the kids taking over the twins. We ate a cold supper, and then Hildi and I cleared the table and did the dishes. Marlies had gone home for the holiday. When all was done, I announced that I would be going to Ulla's party. Father didn't like it. To his mind, I should stay at home on high holy holidays and certainly on Sylvester, to usher in the New Year with family. Mother asked when I would be back. I didn't know. I went into the hallway to put on my coat just as Werner came out of the bathroom. "Where are you going?" he asked with a smirk.

"I've been invited by Ulla."

"Ulla Becker. She has a lot of boyfriends. How about you? Don't you have a boyfriend, too?" With that, and very quickly, he reached under my dress and grabbed my right thigh. I tried to get out of his reach but wasn't fast enough. When he let go, and straightened up, and looked at me with that disgusting smile I had seen before, I slapped him so hard that his glasses went flying. While he searched for them, I left the apartment.

It was easy to forget that nasty interlude in the company of Ulla and her family. She had invited a couple of other girl friends, and Roger came a little later. He was polite and charming as always. Ulla's mother liked him especially, so did Ulla's sister and brother. Ulla's father, who was considerably older than his wife, was a great storyteller. I laughed so much that my cheeks began to ache. As the evening wore on and the old man began telling the stories over again, we laughed even more. Ulla's brother mixed the cocktails and I never knew what I was drinking except that I liked it. By midnight, we stood ready to raise our glasses to cheer the New Year. Roger hugged Ulla and gave her a long kiss. Her parents exchanged a kiss and then opened the wings of a window, leaned way out and shouted into the neighborhood "happy New Year." Many other people did likewise. Fireworks went off in the streets and the bells of the cathedral rang for fifteen minutes. For this special occasion, even Osanna, the largest bell with a wonderfully deep tone, was employed. We four girls, at a signal we had agreed on earlier, pounced with pursed lips on Ulla's younger brother who ran screeching from the room.

It was past midnight when I felt the need to go home. But nobody wanted me to leave. So I stayed another hour. Then, upon rising to leave, Ulla actually locked the apartment door. I didn't really mind. There was more laughter in Ulla's home on that one evening than in my home during the entire year, or so it seemed to me. Every little thing seemed funny. Of course, I knew from other occasions, that it was due to the alcohol. So we drank and laughed some more. Finally, around three-thirty am, she unlocked the door and I left, a little dizzy in the head but otherwise intact. The streets were deserted and silent, the Christmas decorations in the store windows were lit up. It was quite beautiful to be walking about in the still, crisp night. I thought about Leon. How I wished he had come and taken me in his arms and held me close. I wished I had a magic wand that would bring us together, and a magic wand that would secure my future, and a magic wand that would relieve me of all thinking and planning and decision making. Just make things right. But what would be left for me to do, I wondered. And I suddenly remembered how exhilarating it had been for me when I first took life into my own hands, when I planned and decided all by myself and for myself. And I vowed not to forget that again. But what about Leon. Should I write. What if he didn't like me anymore. He still hadn't written, and I feared the worst. Perhaps it was better to keep happily dreaming than to find out a sad truth.

Epiphany, January six, was the secular ending of the Christmas season, and school began the following day. I walked with the boys to their school, and then headed for Paula's house. Hans was in high school now; Hildi would graduate from eighth grade this fall. Her future was another one of those knotty subjects that needed help. The thought occurred to me that Mother might want to make a housemaid of her, as well. Hildi had learning difficulties; it would be a great excuse for Mother to keep her at home. But Hildi was no dummy. And she was very gifted with compassion and intuitiveness. She had a way to sooth the boys when they were fighting, that was quite remarkable. Perhaps the healing arts would be a good place for her. There was another cause for which to fight.

I told Paula that morning that I needed to have a few hours off to attend to something personal. She wanted to know of course, so I told her about my plan to seek some job counseling, if there was such a thing. She would talk with Werner's Mother about a convenient time. Meanwhile, I bathed the babies, fed them, rinsed out the dirty diapers in the toilet, then put them in the special pot with cold water and detergent and put them on the stove. A wood fire would bring them to a boil. Later, I'd wash them out by hand and hang them on a wooden laundry rack in the bathroom, which was heated by a modern oil-fired water heater. Paula had purchased it prior to her wedding.

I had come to feel uneasy in Paula's home since I had knocked the glasses off Werner's face. I hadn't seen him since. And every time I found myself alone, or alone with a baby, I feared that Werner would come in and cause me another problem. Perhaps I should tell Mother or Father about his behavior. Perhaps they could talk with him and make him quit being disgusting. Another problem that needed solving.

Paula told me that I could have Tuesday off, and her mother-in-law would stay with the babies. She mentioned the fact that Werner's glasses got broken on Sylvester and wondered how it happened, since Werner didn't say. I was tempted to say, but thought it better not to. Paula gave me a long look; I feigned ignorance and went about my chores. When I left that evening, in the hallway between shop and home, I could hear Paula and Werner arguing with each other about the broken glasses. I didn't want to be caught overhearing and left quickly.

On the following Tuesday, I went to the school in my neighborhood, where I had spent fifth and sixth grade before entering the business school in Venusbrunn. I spoke with a nun about my needs, and she referred me to someone at the unemployment office. She wrote down the name and wished me good luck. I immediately went to the bureau and asked for Mr. Bittner. After waiting a little while, he came and asked me into his office. He had such an open and sympathetic ear that I spilled out my life's story. He presented me with several options, even some psychological profile tests I might take, if I was unsure about what field to choose. "I really do want to be a governess, but I heard that I'd have to do a three-year apprenticeship; is that so?"

It turned out that since I was eighteen, not fifteen and fresh from the eighth grade, things were a little different. The years I had spent as housekeeper and housemaid and nanny could be counted in lieu of a formal apprenticeship. I felt absolutely elated and fairly squirmed with excitement. Mr. Bittner searched a reference book for the location of the appropriate institute. Beside the one in Hamburg, there was also one in Munich. At the mention of Munich, an exquisite shiver went down my spine. He gave me some forms that my parents and Paula would have to fill out, to show proof of my practical work experience. Then he wrote down the address of the school for me, and I left. I was torn by excitement and worry about the hoops I would have to jump through before Father would agree to my plan.

On my way home, I swung the forms around in my hand like a flag on Independence Day.

That evening, when Mother and Father were watching television, I presented Father with the forms and told him what it was all about. Mother, of course, had a problem with the fact that I was disturbing them in the midst of the show. When she heard what the forms were for, she complained, just as I had anticipated. "You couldn't wait to be working in an office, then you wanted to be a nanny. What makes you think you won't change your mind about being a governess once you start school?"

"I wanted to work in the office because I didn't want to be a housemaid. And Paula asked me to be her nanny; I did it as a favor to her. But I always wanted to be a governess."

"That's news to me."

"Of course. When did you ever ask me what I wanted?"

"Watch your mouth! You're not beyond a slap in the face," she returned with sharp eyes and a threateningly straight posture in her chair.

"Would you please fill out the forms so I can apply to the school," I said.

"What is this going to cost?" Father asked.

"I have no idea, but I'm going to write to the school and find out." Father was watching television; the form lay before him on the table. I said good night and went to bed.

I lay awake for a while, thinking about the school and what it might be like. I would probably enter the school in the fall. I thought about Leon, and I missed him terribly. Neither Father nor Mother had shown any affection to me in a long time, not since childhood, really. It seemed that once we were old enough to have ideas and wishes and, presumably, dreams of our own, my parents' show of affection had ceased. Father still liked to cuddle the little boys, and even Hildi, and they both cooed and cuddled with Paula's babies. Paula had gained respect through her marital status; Walter and Hans were guys and didn't need or want the physical touch. But I yearned for a warm, sincere embrace that wouldn't give up until I had enough. I had done without it now since my birthday in August, and I was becoming desperate. It might have been better not to know Leon, for he had opened to me a window into a way of being that I had never known before. And now, having experienced his loving way, I suffered from missing it.

Life in the New Year quickly settled down into its regular routines. On Saturdays, I went dancing at the base again, and Ulla still hung out with Roger, who continued to bug her about sleeping with him. If you loved me you would show me, was the kind of persuasion he tried. It might have swayed me, if I had been interested in sex at all, for I was rather naive in such things. But Ulla was wise to this nonsense, and it didn't get Roger anywhere.

Walter had completed his apprenticeship in the hardware business and had returned to Hanfurt to take his place as heir apparent. It was nice to have him at home again. He created a lot of fun and laughter because he loved to play with the little boys and with Paula's twins. But conversations at the dinner table, which Mother had usually limited to talk between herself and Father, became more lively, even vociferous, now that Walter was present. Mother did not stifle him in the expression of his views. He had tasted a different social climate in Munich, a large city with an international flair while at the same time preserving the more relaxed atmosphere of the Bavarian character. Father had been a soldier in WWI and had idolized his older brother, John, an officer-to-be who lay dead and buried somewhere in France. Walter, on the other hand, had become intrigued by the pacifists' views of war. Not only that, he had come to admire Chairman Mao's philosophy. Of course, Father rejected anything that didn't agree with his views. Walter, in his youthful enthusiasm, rejected anything that Father stood for. But Walter had a good sense of humor and a willingness to give in without compromising his own beliefs. Peace, sometimes a little shaky, was nonetheless preserved between them.

Father's romantic views of his brother John's officer career, cut very short at the age of twenty-one, came to the fore from time to time. He could not expect Walter to follow in those footsteps, since he needed to take over the family business. But, there was Hans, and even Markus and Matthias, although still way off. And whenever Father talked about his time in the army of Kaiser Wilhelm II, he made sure Hans paid attention. I never knew just what Hans heard or did not hear; he had such a remarkable way of tuning out whatever didn't interest him. He could face the speaker with eyes wide open and presumably awake; yet his mind, and thereby his ears, were tuned to other stations. He was kind and helpful, and often read to the little boys from his books of science fiction. Then he was glad to answer any questions the boys had. He had a wonderful way of explaining things by comparing the matter of discussion to things of daily life, which the little guys could understand. And he never talked down to them. He would make a great teacher, I thought. Yet Father seemed to see him only as a future army officer.

On one of my Saturdays at the army base, I met a new soldier by the name of Jack. He seemed a little older than most other GIs. He was a handsome, outgoing guy who knew quite a bit of German. Consequently, we had some real conversations, not the kinds of talk that constantly broke down, because one or the other had failed to understand. We danced a great deal together, and, perhaps because of it, no other GI came to ask me. Frau Mueller reminded me of the rules. I told Jack what was expected, and so he sat out the next dance. One of the regulars asked me to dance, and then Jack was back again. He came from Montana, way out in the hinterland, he said. He told me the most enchanting stories about his way of life and the beauty of the land where he lived. His family owned horses, and he could ride them any time he wanted; ride across wide-open spaces with the wind in his hair, sunshine on his face, and nothing to stop him. They would go by horse into the mountains to cut their own Christmas tree and the horses seemed to love the snow as well as people did. Hearing his stories of life with horses reminded me of a childhood dream, long forgotten, of doing exactly that which he had described so vividly.

A horse. I had wanted a horse, and around the age of ten I had told Father about it. We were walking somewhere in the neighborhood when I told him. Father said he would get me one. "Today is Tuesday," he said and thought for a moment, then added, "by Thursday you will have a horse." I was old enough to know that we had no place to keep a horse, and I asked him how he would do it. He just smiled and said, "trust me." I figured, Father knows best, so I trusted him. Thursday morning, when I woke up, Father and Mother, Erna and Paula, all with big smiles on their faces, were gathered in my bedroom, and Father pointed to a rocking horse and said, "there is your horse." I never again believed anything he said.

Jack had very dark brown eyes and a quick and easy-going smile. His dark hair was cut GI style, very short. He had full, inviting lips, a square jaw and tiny ears for his large face. I could go for him, crossed my mind. When our togetherness became a problem for me, and Frau Mueller commented on it, Jack suggested that we meet outside the club. It was just for conversation, I thought, and agreed. Since I didn't want to be totally alone with him, I asked Ulla to bring Roger and make it a double date. Ulla agreed. We met at Café Braun at three o'clock. When I reached the Café, Jack was already there. He got up to greet me, then we looked for a table for four, and pretty soon Ulla and Roger showed up. The guys didn't know each other; one was from company A, the other from company B. After introductions, to which Jack spoke German, Ulla and I ordered coffee and cake, the guys asked for beer. It seemed to me that Roger took a dislike to Jack. Later on, Ulla revealed that Roger thought it pretentious of Jack to speak to him in German. Jack was his usual friendly, outgoing self, and the two guys exchanged some military news.

Ulla smiled at me and said, "he's cute."

"You know," I replied, "It's uncanny; he likes everything that I like. And he has horses at home in Montana. Horses! How I wanted to have a horse!"

"You got that from the Westerns you used to watch."

"Right. But I still want a horse, or at least to ride one. I had forgotten about it."

"Well, maybe now you'll have a chance."

"Oh, don't be stupid," I said, knowing full well what she was hinting at. "But what about you?"

"I don't want a horse," she said and laughed.

"Oh, stop it! You know what I mean."

"Roger wants to marry me," Ulla said calmly and smiled.

"Did you have sex with him?"

"Noo," she said, impatient with my line of questioning. "He'll have to marry me first."

"How can you hold out so long? Maybe you don't really care to have sex, do you?"

"Well, that, too. But I also want it to be a beautiful experience, and there really isn't anywhere that we could make it that. I can't do it at home, and can't do it at the base. He would have to rent a hotel room, I suppose. But I don't like that either. Seems so cheap, you know. So, we might as well wait until we are married."

"What about your parents? Do they know things have gotten this serious?"

"They'd have to be blind not to see it. But my father hasn't said anything. So, I don't really know what he's thinking."

"And your Mother?"

"Oh, she'd like it just fine if I lived in the US. She'd have a reason to fly."

Jack and I met again the following Saturday at the same Café. Afterward, we went for a long walk around Hanfurt. It was getting dark by the time I reached home. We stopped across the street in a secluded spot to say goodnight. Jack suddenly took me into his arms and kissed me. He held me so tight, and his mouth held my mouth so hard that I could not get away. No matter what I tried, I could not get out of his grip. It dawned on me what it must be like to be raped. I was scared. When he finally released me, I just ran. "What's the matter?" I heard him calling after me. "Didn't you like it?"

Hildi, of course, knew right away that something unpleasant had happened. She sat up in bed, didn't say a word, but looked at me silently and waited for an explanation. My mouth ached. I checked it in a mirror and saw that Jack had actually damaged my lips. "This guy just literally chewed on me," I said to Hildi.

"He did what?"

"He kissed me, except he kissed me so hard that he bit my lips, see?" and I moved closer to Hildi so she could see better.

"He really did. Are you going to see him again?"

"No way. What's more, he didn't even ask me, you know, come on slowly so that I could let him know if I wanted to be kissed or not. You're lucky. All you have to do is look at a guy with your third eye and you'll know if he's worth your time or not."

I didn't wash my face or brush my teeth that night; I just fell into bed and cried for Leon.

"Poor Fannie," I heard Hildi mumble.

Ulla called me a few days later to see if I'd like to go to a movie. "And I have something important to tell you," she said.

"Well, tell me now," I said.

"No. Let's meet at the theater at seven, and then I'll tell you."

"I have something to tell you, too. Okay, tomorrow night at seven."

We met as planned, bought our tickets and went inside to find good seats in the half-light of the movie house. We sat down, and then Ulla said, "you go first." I told her what had happened with Jack.

"Wow! He must really like you."

"Are you crazy? If what he did was because he liked me, I hate to think what he would do if he loved me."

"Oh, I suppose. Was it your first kiss?"

"No. Leon was the first one. He was so gentle and so sweet. Just wonderful. If this Jack jerk – hah! Jack jerk, jerk Jack, jerky Jack," we laughed. "If this jerk had been the first one, it would have scared me away for life. But, what's your important thing?"

"He's married."

"Who?"

"Jack. Roger found out that Jack is married."

"That bastard!" I nearly yelled it. Feelings of outrage over his utter disrespect, and frustration over unrequited revenge, created such an inner turmoil in me that I could hardly concentrate on the movie. Only one thing gave me a measure of satisfaction: the resolve to slap him across the face should I ever happen to see him again. "That bastard!"

"Believe it or not, there's a good side to this," said Ulla. "You might have kept seeing him, and who knows how it might have ended, huh?"

"You're right. What a jerk!"

It was time to bring up the matter of the forms that Father needed to fill out for me. I was nervous about it. Asking for anything was like pulling teeth, first from one, then from the other of my parents. I had received the forms from school, including everything else I needed to know. I had written everything down for Father, and had waited for his response, which, as usual, did not come. One morning, before going to work for Paula, I stopped in at his office and asked about the forms.

"The forms?" he said, and his forehead wrinkled up.

"Yes, the forms that you need to fill out about my work experience, remember?"

"Hmm," he grumbled, and his eyes looked around his desk. "I think they're upstairs."

"Where upstairs, Dad?"

"On the table where you left them, I guess."

"No," I said. "They're not there. Are you sure you left them upstairs? Then I'll go looking for them." I left the office, worried that Mother might have torn them to bits and flushed them down the toilet. Paula had already filled out her set of forms and had sent them back. That evening, after returning home, I began looking all over the apartment. I asked the kids if they had seen any, asked Marlies and Mother, thumbed through old newspapers and magazines, but they had disappeared. Rather than waste any more time, I wrote to the school, apologized for the misplaced papers, and asked for another set of forms. They came within a few days, and then I sat down and filled them out myself. There was next to nothing I couldn't handle; it bugged me that I hadn't done it the first time. All that was left to do was for Father to sign.

Again, on a morning before leaving for work, I went to his office with the completed forms. "Dad," I said, "they're all filled out. You just need to sign them."

"Sign what?"

"The application forms for the Pedagogical Institute in Munich. They have an opening for me and I can start classes in September." I laid them down on his desk before him.

Father's face wrinkled up in folds of irritation. I had expected it and stood firm. He pushed the forms aside and said, "not now, I'm busy."

"You're always busy Dad, too busy to spend any time or thought on us kids." I took care to say it calmly. Father looked up and I expected a torrent of rebuke. He looked me in the face. I held his gaze. Then he looked down on his desk and said, " I'll have to talk to your Mother first." I took the forms, to keep them from getting lost again and went off to work.

Paula was more eager to hear about my plans. She was happy for me even though she worried about finding help with the babies. "I would have loved to be a PE teacher," she said. "I would be independent and not have to rely on a husband for a living," she mused. I sensed from the look on her face that she was not happy.

"But you have two beautiful babies," I pointed out, thinking that they would be a consolation for her.

"Yes, I do, but it's not good enough. Babies make you feel special for a while, but they don't give you any self-esteem or pride in something you're really good at. Sure, I've accomplished something by giving birth, but that sensation soon fades with all the work that's involved. Besides, it's my body that produced the babies. I wasn't even asked. But if I were a teacher I'd have an education, learned and probably seen many things, have a title, and be somebody. Now, I'm just somebody's wife, and not even a special somebody's wife."

"And you could get a divorce," I suddenly added. Heaven only knew what made me say that, but looking at Paula showed me that I had touched a chord. She said nothing and left the room.

Father did not sign the forms that evening. I had to prod him into discussing it with Mother. Mother became rather hostile that more money was to be spent on me simply because I wanted to learn something knew. She figured that I had a career and didn't need a second one.

"Do you know why I wanted to go to school in Venusbrunn?" I asked her.

"Because Erna had gone," she said with great conviction.

"No, that's not why. I had read a book about a girl in boarding school. She had a lot of fun there, and I thought I could have a lot of fun, too. That's why I wanted to go."

Mother looked down and was silent for a moment. Then she said, "your grades weren't good enough for you to continue in school. You would have had to repeat the sixth grade."

"I wonder why," I remarked and nearly choked with anguish at her statement. At the age of five, I was going to day care, a noisy, crowded, disorganized place where I felt utterly lost. So every day, when Walter came home from school, I sat down beside him and copied his homework. I wanted to go to school, too. So halfway into the school year, my parents talked to the principal and it was agreed that I should be entered on trial. If I could not keep up with the other children, I could always repeat the first grade. I loved the order and regularity of school life and not only kept up, but even surpassed some of the other girls. Yet by the time I had reached the sixth grade I was a failure. Did she never ask herself what had gone wrong?

Father said they would talk about it. I knew that routine. In the end, each one would refer me to the permission of the other one, but the other one never had the nerve to say yes. I would have to wait for the right moment to trick Father into it.

Father's birthday was coming soon. It happened to fall just before Ash Wednesday that year, right into the high life of the Fasching season (the weeks before the beginning of Lent). It was not just any birthday, but his sixtieth. Ten years earlier, life was just emerging from a devastating war, and the gifts had been few and meager. Things were better now, and Father planned a grand dinner in a distinguished restaurant for the family and all the employees. Hildi was getting excited. She would have a chance to see Jordan, from the sales department. He had completed his apprenticeship in Father's business and was now a full-fledged salesman of appliances. He would be at the dinner, and Hildi dreamed of sitting beside him. I thought I might try to make it possible. I could set myself down between him and whoever else, and after dinner and some drinking, and before or during the impromptu entertainment that was sure to follow, I would wander off and let Hildi take my place. I told Hildi of my plan. She would keep an eye on me and quickly fill my vacant seat before someone else got the notion to do so.

I was rather looking forward to the dinner myself. Father employed around fifty people, the great majority of them men of varying ages. Some of them had been part of the company before Father married Mother. They had become an extended family to us children: the older women as motherly friends, the young women as girl-friends, the older men represented a fatherly image, and the young men – well, between them and us girls there had always been lots of romantic ogling.

On the night of the dinner, Mother, Father, Hans, and Hildi drove to the banquet. Walter and I walked. He was half a head taller than I and had a nice even gait. I put my arm into his; he was old enough not to mind it anymore. I told him of my plans for the fall. When we reached the hall, most of the employees had already arrived. Walter sat down at the head table where Father, Mother, Paula, and Werner, as well as a couple of company hotshots, were seated. Hans preferred sitting with the delivery drivers, with whom he had gone on tour from time to time. Next to Jordan sat a young woman from the typing pool I was friends with. I asked her quietly if she would let me sit beside Jordan for a while. She obliged me. I sat down on his right side, on his left side sat the assistant bookkeeper, Frau Schulze.

During dinner it was fairly quiet. Father wore his tailcoat. Having been a soldier once, properly erect posture was important to him, and any time he caught us slouching or leaning on something or with hands in pockets, he was quick to correct us. Mother wore a new black dress that had some lace on the bodice, and a string of pearls around her neck. She was a big woman but well proportioned. She never wore make-up, but had a naturally smooth complexion. She never even had acne, which is something all of us girls had become well acquainted with. I could see that she was enormously pleased with the event and the exposure it gave her. I knew from experience that my parents became rather tolerant at these affairs. While they insisted on perfect behavior anywhere in the office or the store, and could never forgive even a minor transgression brought on simply by youthful thoughtlessness, yet at an event such as the banquet, major birthday parties, costume balls during Fasching and the like, whenever many people were around, they seemed to see and hear nothing reprehensible. Were they not watching? Did Father not care? Did Mother enjoy herself so much that she didn't want her pleasure spoiled by parental duties? I never knew.

A costume ball was going on in an adjacent large dance hall, and the music drifted in to us at just the right volume. After dinner, the impromptu entertainment began. Jokes and skits, some by employees, some by long-time acquaintances, and some by Walter, were presented and caused much amusement. The oldest member of the company had known Father for nearly forty years, and he presented a hilarious account of Father's years as a young sales agent on the road. The brass band of a merchant organization, of which Father was a member, serenaded him. When everyone stood up with champagne in hand to toast Father, I felt very proud of the distinguished figure that he posed in his well-fitting tailcoat. Meanwhile, beer and wine flowed readily. I talked with Jordan who wanted to hear about my East German border escapades all the while he was ogling Hildi. And I chatted with Frau Schulze who was also a long-time employee. She related how she had always wondered how we children managed never to fall down any of the many stairs on our way to the flat roof, because we always ran - we never walked anywhere. We ran through the office at top-speed, ripped open the doors coming and going, and shot out into the loading yard without ever running into a truck, all the while laughing and shouting and trying to be first on the roof. She knew everyone that I knew; we were an extended family.

I felt it was time to give Hildi a chance and I stood up. She noticed right away and came over. "Hildi," I said so that Jordan could hear it. "Save my seat for me, would you. I need to stretch a bit." With that I left and Hildi sat down, a little shy but looking quite happy.

I went to the restroom through the dance hall where the costume party was going on. Some people had complete costumes that one could recognize as a particular character; some wore regular clothes and just donned a funny hat. Young women wore such skimpy outfits as would never be allowed in ordinary settings, and the same was true with behavior. Smoking, drinking, and making out took place everywhere, including the stairwell to the upper floor. Then I noticed that some of our people had begun to mingle with the costumed dancers.

I sat down at one of the tables for a while and watched them moving in and out. I could see Werner with a lecherous look on his face, as his eyes scanned the tables for victims, I figured. When he came and asked me to dance I told him to dance with his wife. He didn't seem swayed and just went to one of the office girls and asked her. She agreed. I watched them, and it didn't take long for Werner to snap her brassiere. With a jerk of annoyance, she turned away from him and sat down again. I didn't know if Paula had noticed. She was chatting with the company buyer, a long-time employee. Not only was he an employee, he was also a friend. During the war, when the allies were bombing Hanfurt, Erna and Paula had lived with his family for a while.

Then Hermann noticed me. Gorgeous Hermann with blue eyes, blond hair, rosy cheeks and crooked legs. Five years earlier, on a company bus day-tour, Hermann and I had been hanging out together. Perhaps I had followed him around, or maybe he had followed me around. I never really knew. During a stop in a small town, and not being interested in sightseeing, we wondered off and came to a wooded area beside a road. At the edge of the wood we found a swing suspended from one of the trees, and Hermann started swinging. He noticed that the rope on one side was frayed and he asked me to look for something to mend it, like a wire or such. I looked a little, but I had no real interest. What I wanted was to swing. Finally, he got off and I got on. A convertible with the roof down and four people in it was driving by as I started swinging. I watched the people, who were watching me and craned their necks to not lose sight of me. I kept wondering why they kept watching me. When the road turned and the car vanished from sight, I found myself sitting on the ground, where I had fallen when the rope gave way.

Hermann asked me to dance. He was a good dancer, and I enjoyed his company. We moved back and forth from the dining hall to the dance hall. He recalled the event with the swing and we laughed about it. "You know," he whispered into my ear, "I always liked you."

"Why didn't you tell me?"

"How could I?"

"Well, you open your mouth, scrunch you lips and tongue into a certain configuration…"

Herman laughed. "I had no idea that's how you do it." We giggled.

"But really, how come you never said anything to me about it. We see each other often enough."

"Oh, I couldn't, you being the boss' daughter. You remember Lauer, who liked your sister Erna?" I nodded. "You know what the other guys called him? Gold digger."
"And that's why he never made a move?"

"That's right."

"Oh, poor Erna. She really liked him a lot. And I was so mean to her."

It was way past midnight by now. Father and Mother had taken Hildi and Hans home. Some of the employees had left also, but the majority stayed with the crowd and kept dancing. A couple of the other guys from the company danced with me, and then Hermann was back for more. He bought me drinks, and I became ever more enamored of him. It was past four o'clock in the morning when I decided to go home and Hermann offered to walk with me. When we reached my house, I unlocked the downstairs door and entered the long, dark hallway. Hermann followed me. The street lantern shed a little yellow light through the wrought-iron grill of the door window. I leaned my hot face against the cool wall, thinking of Leon and wishing him to be here now. Instead it was Hermann who took me into his arms and kissed me, a long gentle kiss. I pretended it was Leon and kissed him back. Hermann held me close and long, and kept kissing me, but when his kisses became wilder and his body pressed ever harder into mine, I pushed him away.

"You better go now," I said. Hermann looked at me as though this had been a game for him, to see just how far he could get with the boss' daughter. Then he smiled good-naturedly and kissed me once more gently on the cheek and left. I locked the door and went upstairs. Hildi was asleep. She would tell me tomorrow how it went with Jordan.

On the next regular working day I went to the office to talk with Eleanor, a girl from the typing pool in Father's office. She often took dictation from Father, then the typed letters were placed, one at a time, between the blotting pages of a special folder. Then Father signed them one by one.

I didn't reveal to her my plan so as not to get her in trouble, but I asked that she give me the folder before taking it to Father. Eleanor agreed. I placed the form that needed signing behind a letter, matching the signature space of the letter with that of the form. A small bit of tape held the two papers together, and a little piece of carbon paper between them in the right spot would cause Father's signature to copy through to the form. Eleanor took the folder to Father who looked over the letters and signed them. Then she brought the folder back to me. It had worked like a charm! His signature was exactly where it should be. Overjoyed, I folded the form and mailed it off. I still had the post office box that I had rented after returning from Wiesenthal.

A few weeks later, I received a registration notice from the Pedagogical Institute, including all the other information that I would need. Classes would begin on the fifth of

September. By that time I needed to find a place to live. Munich, like so many other German cities, had been heavily bombed during WWII. Not only that, but it had also seen a great influx of refugees from the East, with the result that a housing shortage existed for many years to come. But Walter had lived there several years; surely he could help me find a place. All I needed was one room.

Walter didn't spend much time at home; when he wasn't working, he went out with friends. When he was just fifteen, Mother used to send Erna to the Gasthaus to find him and bring him home. He'd be sitting with much older guys, smoking, drinking beer, and playing cards. I used to fear that he would never amount to anything. But Walter was a good guy.

The next time I saw him, I told him of my plan and what I needed. Walter resembled Erna a lot, but I didn't mind because he was more fun. He had a great sense of humor, while Erna had been a sourpuss. He was in a hurry to go somewhere, but he waited long enough to hear me out. "Just what do you think is going to happen when Dad gets a bill from that Institute?" he asked me, astonished at my actions with the signature.

"I don't know, and I don't care. I have to do this. Dad is going to find out soon enough, I suppose. In the meantime, don't you tell anybody," I warned him.

"Well, it's not my problem. So, what do you want?"

"Tell me how I can find a room near the school."

"What's the address?" I read it to him from the registration form. "Hmm. That's not anywhere near where I used to live. But give me some time and I'll look into it. Gotta go now." With that he rushed off, then suddenly stopped, turned around and asked, "whatever became of your boyfriend, Leon? Is he still around?"

"He's in Munich," I answered with a grin.

"Aha!" he shouted back in my direction as he ran down the stairs.

I went to the kitchen to get something to drink and heard Mother and Hildi talking about dancing class. "You and Hans can take the course together," she said.

Hildi let out a wail. "Not with Hans. It's embarrassing."

"Well it's with him or not at all," Mother said firmly.

Hildi looked at me, her face contorted in anguish at the thought she would have to go dancing with her brother. I motioned her to follow me. Once in our room, I said, "don't worry about it. You don't have to dance with Hans. There will be plenty of other guys, and I bet Hans wouldn't want to dance with you either. Just be glad she said yes. You remember the trouble I had just getting her permission?" Hildi nodded. "By the way, how are things with Jordan?"

Hildi smiled blissfully. "Every time I go through the sales office he looks and smiles at me. Wouldn't it be great if he would take the same dance course as me?"

"That would be great. But don't get your hopes up, Hildi. Once upon a time, Erna was crazy about Lauer from the warehouse. Hermann told me that Lauer liked her too, but the other guys called him a gold digger. He didn't have the nerve to make a move, and Erna never had a chance to be with him. There'll be lots of other guys, so cheer up."

"Poor Erna," Hildi said and looked so sad that I was reminded of my part in the disaster that killed Erna, and the sting of guilt was most painful.

"Then again," I said, "tell him that you're taking classes. Maybe he'll enroll too, who knows." Hildi was sitting on the chair by her bed, and my suggestion drew her mouth into a smile of hope and delight. I left her musing about the possibilities.

Neither Ulla nor I went dancing at the base again. She wanted to spend her time with Roger, and I didn't want to run into Jack. Whenever I had a chance, I went by her shop, and if she wasn't busy, we talked. I found out from her one day that

Roger would be going back to the States in August. August fifteenth, to be precise.

"We're engaged," she told me one sunny day in June, and she showed me her golden wedding band, worn on the left hand to signify engagement. It looked rather cheap to me, but I said nothing.

"He's going to give me his mother's diamond ring once we get to the States," she said. " This is just a cheapy, and temporary." She appeared to be very happy, and I congratulated her, despite my reservations about the limited time that she had known him. What did she, could she really know about him whom she never saw in company with others, around his family, under circumstances other than just going steady. What kind of work would he be doing after getting back to the states. Was he catholic or something else. I didn't want do bother her with all that, though. It wasn't my problem anyway.

We met after work at the Italian ice cream parlor where she explained her problem to me: how to convince her parents to let her go. She was not yet twenty-one, but wanted to leave together with Roger. He claimed to have started the paper work. She seemed indeed very much in love with him. Had she had sex with him, I wondered. At one point in our conversation she seemed to catch on to my unspoken question because she suddenly shook her head as she burst out with, "nooo, we didn't have sex." I grinned, she grinned. But he was still pressing her for it.

She called me two week later and asked me to meet her at the Café after work. She sounded upset, and I worried about her. When she came to the Café her eyes were red from crying.

"What's the matter, Ulla?"

"He's gone."

"Who is gone?"

"Roger."

"Roger left? Back to the States?"

"He lied to me," Ulla said and the tears began to flow. "He lied about everything, and the worst thing is…" and now she sobbed uncontrollably. The waitress came and I ordered coffee and pastries. After Ulla had calmed down a little, she continued, "the worst thing is that he finally talked me into having sex. It's like that's all he ever wanted. Not me. Just sex."

I felt so bad for her that I put my arm around her and held her while she cried. It was quite a while before she calmed down enough to where we could talk about how it happened. Roger had borrowed a car from a friend and had taken Ulla out into the country for a picnic. They had found a secluded spot where he spread a blanket, and after eating, they lay down a while. The sky was blue, the birds were singing, the sun was warm – one thing led to another, and it happened. The saddest part of it was that, although their lovemaking had been very enjoyable at the time, his ugly betrayal destroyed it in retrospect.

What's the matter with guys, I wondered. Werner had a wife but couldn't keep his hands off other women. Jack just took it for granted that I wanted him. But Roger was a real scoundrel. To play this game of cat and mouse for such a long time, and so thoroughly as to buy a wedding band for no other reason than for the sake of the chase! I would never have believed it possible that such people exist. I thought of Leon and his gentle and caring ways, and I missed him terribly.

The twins were almost one year old now and needed a lot of attention since they were starting to walk. Keeping them from falling and bumping into furniture and grabbing forbidden items while each one headed in a different direction became very trying. But I had promised Paula I would stay with them until I had to leave for Munich, and she had filled out the forms accordingly.

It was on the day of the twins' first birthday that Father and Mother came for the customary birthday visit. That's when Paula brought up the fact that I would be leaving in September. I sensed that she had done it on purpose, because she knew as well as I, that in the presence of Werner und his mother, and a couple of elderly aunts, our parents would be less confrontational. Father voiced a staccatoed "hm!" but did not cause a scene. Mother put on her most polished smile and didn't let on that she hadn't known. They learned that day, how I had acquired Father's signature on the form, which listed my experiences, and extolled my virtues as housekeeper and child caregiver. Paula joined in by telling, that she had filled out her part of the forms that referred to my work as a nanny. She had done this for me gladly, and wished me success. That's when I made it known that classes would begin on the fifth of September.

Werner's Mother and his aunts had not heard about my plans and were curious to learn more. Especially Werner's aunt, Maria, who had been a professional photographer before retirement, cheered me on. For being an old lady, she had a great sense of humor and enthusiasm for life. She had never been married, and had owned her own business. Perhaps that was the reason why she had not dried up like so many other old people I knew, who seemed to be dead while still walking around. It was a great relief for me that it finally came out in the open. I spent that evening with Ulla so that I could stay away until late, and not get home until Father and Mother were watching the late news. But my calculations did not add up. When I said a hasty goodnight, Mother called me in. I stood before them like a poor sinner, while they took turns raging at me. The only way to deal with these hysterics was to tune them out. I had always done this by keeping my eyes focused on the rug to study the oriental pattern. But it was a vain attempt. Besides, the fear of getting a beating with the wooden clothes hanger, or the broomstick, kept me on edge, all the while they vented their fury. Not one thought did they give to my reason, or need, for doing what I had done. I was just simply a bad person, disobedient, a liar and therefore also a thief, ashamed of my siblings, running the streets like a bitch in heat… on and on. There I stood, in a room filled with venom, stoically and silently waiting until their frustration had spent itself. Once in bed, though, the ugliness of it all brought out the tears and I cried for Leon who was so gentle and kind and loving. I decided right there and then to find him again.

The next time I saw Walter, I asked him what he could advise me to do. Walter had forgotten what I asked him. I repeated it and he promised not to forget this time. But rather than depend on him alone, I wrote to the school asking for help in finding a room, or boarding house, or the like.

Whenever I addressed an envelope to Munich, my insides began to tingle. Once there, I would look for Leon. Surely the phonebook would have the address of his brother's butchery beside the phone number. Should I go and see him there, I wondered. Or would it be better to write first. What if he didn't care about me anymore. What actually happened, I wondered, the last time we were together. I recalled that Leon had shouted as the border guards took me away, "don't worry, I'll call your parents." And I remembered shouting back, "Noo!" And then I remembered that puzzled look on his face. But there had been something else in that expression as well, something like an exclamation point, as though he had just thought 'Aha!' And there had been sadness and resignation, too. And suddenly, I realized, that Leon had understood what I had not admitted to myself: that his profession as butcher was a problem for me. But it was only because of my parents and how they would think of him, I thought. But it was useless. I knew I couldn't fool myself any longer. It was me, no one else, who had the problem.

It was devastating to see how stupid I had been. This wonderful guy had slipped through my fingers, because I didn't like that he was a butcher. My parents would consider him inferior, my parents, who treated me like an inferior, and made me fight for every little right and privilege that should have been mine by nature. Oh God! I could have kicked myself. Fear that I might be too late gripped me. Should I write to him? Was it better not to? Should I wait till I saw him in person? I couldn't decide. All I could do was hope.

Hildi graduated from eighth grade in July. I often talked with her about her future, and, much to my delight, she told me that she wants to be a nurse. At a friendlier occasion, I told my parents about it. Father shrugged and voiced a staccatoed "hm!" Mother pointed out that her grades had not been good, and she doubted that Hildi had what it took to succeed with further study. Her love of children and babies would give her the drive to succeed, I pointed out, but Mother did not agree.

Then I thought about the boys, and what they would want for themselves. I thought it a good idea to foster in them the notion that they had a right to choose. So, one day, we all sat down together, and I asked each one. Hans, who was now seventeen, had his eyes on space technology. Markus, who would be eleven in November, loved to build things. And Matthias, with his left arm week from the polio that had struck him as a baby, wanted to be a teacher. Hildi talked again about being a nurse, and the four became rather animated, and joked and laughed together about their imagined exploits as adults.

Marlies was still with us, and I asked her one day if she had plans to stay in our household. She admitted that she would continue with her employment. But one day in early August, Marlies went home on leave and never returned. "What happened?" I asked Mother.

"Never you mind," Mother said and pushed me aside. And just as she had done with me, she proceeded to tell Hildi what kinds of chores to do. Hildi looked at me with alarm. She understood what was in store for her. We would talk about it later, I whispered to her.

That evening, I told her, "looks like you're going to have a fight on your hands, just like me."

"I wish I could go with you to Munich. I want to get out of here."

"Be patient, Hildi. You will."

"Walter and Hans can have careers, and Father has even asked the little guys what they want to be. But nobody asks us girls. We're just told what to do, like it or not," and Hildi, who had been pacing in anger, kicked the furniture and hurt her foot in the process. "For Paula she has respect, maybe it's because she's a business man's wife, with little kids to take care of, just like her."

"I think so. Before Paula was married, she got the same treatment as you and me. I suspect that she married Werner to get away from home. He was probably the only one who asked her. I think we all try to escape in one way or other. Walter escapes to his friends, Hans escapes to his books, and," it suddenly occurred to me, "you escape to bed, don't you?" Hildi nodded.

"That's why I go to bed so early," she said.

"Women have always been controlled by men, but it's beginning to change. Look at it this way: be the housemaid for a while; it won't hurt you to learn a few things about how to run a household. It saved me three years of an apprenticeship. Once you feel ready, and you're mature enough, you'll take things into your own hands, and you'll win. Meanwhile, you still have the boys around, and they're fun, aren't they?"

Hildi's face lit up. "Yeah, they are. And I have some friends from school that I can do things with."

"I didn't even have that for a long time," I said.

"And if Mother thinks I'm too young to go out alone, I can ask Hans to go with me. In September, we'll start dancing classes. I really look forward to that."

"And you even have Walter to help you. He was not at home when I was in your shoes."

"Poor Fannie," Hildi said, and she hugged and kissed me.

"You have to write to me and fill me in on everything that happens."

I turned twenty in August; another year gone by which Leon and I would not celebrate together. The closer it got to September, the more nervous I became. Excitement over seeing Leon again, and the fear that it might be too late, plagued my insides to near nausea. I had to concentrate hard on other things to avoid the sickening consequences of this inner conflict. Through his acquaintances, Walter had been able to find me a room near the school. I had bought whatever clothes I would need and a large enough suitcase, all of it with my own earnings. It gave me a great sense of accomplishment. Not only that, but it also made me feel as though I had finally arrived in that privileged realm of adulthood. That age, which children dream about, when one can have what, when, and how one wants it, or so it seemed to the child then.

Ulla and I got together on the last Sunday of August. Ingrid came too, and we went swimming at the public swimming pool, with its great expanse of lawns where people sunned themselves under a rare cloudless sky, or played badminton. From the pool, we walked to the Hanfurt river, which made up one stretch of border around the otherwise fenced pool property. Then we had some ice cream at the outdoor pool café, still enjoying the cloudless sky and very warm sun. Ulla had gotten over Roger, even felt somewhat relieved at not having to fight it out with her parents about leaving for the U.S. Ingrid still worked at the bank. She had recently completed her apprenticeship, which required, besides on-the-job training, one day per week of academic schooling. She was now earning a good salary as a banker. Ulla and Ingrid planned to go dancing together at the base again, but this time they vowed to obey the rules.

My last day at work came. I knew I would miss the babies, and I was sure the feeling was mutual. Paula and I had grown closer during the past year than we had ever been before. She had a gift for me: a beautiful emerald green sweater she had knitted with mohair wool. It fit like a glove. Her Mother-in-law had enjoyed my company, she said and gave me a cosmetic travel case for a going-away present. Werner came over to say good-bye. Since I had slapped him in the face he had been on his best behavior around me.

Then came the great day, the first of September. I had packed my bags and had bought my train ticket the previous day. Nearly unbearable tension made me feel ill. As the little boys, who were not so little anymore, stood ready to go to school, I kissed and hugged them and promised to be back for Christmas. Then I shook hands with Walter, who had to get back to the office. With a twinkle in his eyes, he wished me good luck. Hans and Hildi would walk me to the station that was only three blocks away. Then I shook hands with Mother. Mother had tears in her eyes; it surprised me. Was it possible that Mother was sad to see me go? Perhaps she wished she could go also. For years, she and Father had never gone on a vacation. First the war, then lack of money, and ever more babies had made it impossible. Finally, when times had grown better, they had taken a trip to Rome. I came to think that it had awakened in Mother a hankering for more travel. Maybe she envied me for having a career, something that had not been possible for her. Perhaps it had caused her much unhappiness, which she had let out on us children. She gave me a book that she had bought for me, one volume of many by my favorite author of adventure stories. I was touched. Then Mother hugged me rather stiffly; she felt like an ironing board in my arms, and we said good-bye.

I went downstairs to Father's office while Hans and Hildi tended my luggage. Father stood up from his desk, and with a self-conscious smile, he voiced his standard advice, "remember where you come from!" and, "keep your distance."

"The School and my landlady will send monthly bills; I hope that agrees with you?" Father nodded.

"You'll need some taxi money when you get to Munich." With that, he reached into his pocket and pulled out a fairly large amount of money. And with his characteristic sheepish grin, he asked, "is that enough?"

It made me laugh, and I answered, "yes Dad, it's plenty."

He handed it to me and said, "If you need anything, you know what to do." We shook hands, and then I turned and left his office. I thought about all the other times I had left his office in fear or agony over something I needed, inwardly shaking, hoping to be able to see the matter through. What a relief it was that I would never have to feel that way again.

I caught up with Hans and Hildi who had made their way slowly toward the station. Once there, and before going through the turnstile to the platform, I shook hands with Hans who smiled bashfully but stood tall and erect. "Look out for Hildi," I said to him.

"I will," he said, loud and clear as though he was exchanging marriage vows. I laughed.

Then I hugged and kissed Hildi who had tears in her eyes, and I said, "remember what we talked about. Time will pass quickly, you'll see. And don't forget to write and let me know what happens. Anyhow, I'll be home for Christmas vacation. That's just a few weeks." Hildi nodded.

"Are you going to look for Leon?" she asked then with a big grin, as though she had a stake in my happiness.

"I sure will, and if I find him, and if he still cares for me, I'll bring him home for Christmas, that's a promise." Hildi giggled with joy. Then I picked up my luggage, went past the ticket window, and walked to the platform where my train for Munich pulled up a few minutes later.

By mid-afternoon I arrived in Munich, queasier than ever. A taxi driver spied me as soon as I came out of the terminal and offered his services. I gave him the address, he stowed my luggage and off we went. I looked out the window and caught myself hoping I'd see Leon. How silly of me. Compared to Hanfurt, Munich was an immense sea of buildings, and cars, and people, and in that constantly moving and shifting picture I could not possibly hope to find a glimpse of Leon.

My future home happened to be a very nice large room on the third floor of a neo-classical apartment building that had either never been damaged by bomb shrapnel or else had been repaired. The apartment belonged to Frau Schuessler, a widow of about seventy who lived alone and needed extra income. My room was situated in such a way that I could come and go without disturbing her. There was a bed, nightstand and wardrobe set from the previous century, and a table with two matching chairs. I would share the bathroom with my landlady.

I was anxious to go out and find Leon, but I had to wait. Frau Schuessler made coffee, it was very good, and we sat down on the sofa in the living room to discuss the rules of living under her roof. She would provide bed sheets and towels, breakfast and supper; dinner was on me. She was acquainted with the people where Walter had lived. Apparently he had made a good impression there, and so Frau Schuessler had been quick to accept me on their request. She was a stout woman, not very tall, with long gray hair that she wrapped around her head in a most peculiar, but attractive way. She wore a pink organza blouse with puffy sleeves. I had never seen a woman of her age in pink, much less organza, and it made me think that this lady would have humor and enthusiasm and would be fun to be around. Later, we had supper together, and then I went to my room and unpacked my suitcase. I stowed away my clothes and checked out the bed; it promised to be comfortable, squeaky, but comfortable. In order to keep from thinking about Leon and getting sick from the tension, I began reading the book Mother had given me. But I couldn't concentrate, and I went to sleep instead. The sooner I slept, the sooner the next day would arrive.

By six o'clock I was wide awake. After breakfast at half past seven, I went out. Frau Schuessler had given me a set of keys, one for downstairs, the other for the apartment door. I had checked the phonebook for a butcher shop by the name of Kramer and written down the address. Frau Schuessler explained to me the public transportation system. After some trials and errors, and boarding wrong busses, or right busses in the wrong direction, I finally made it to the central railroad station. From there I took a taxi to the Kramer butcher shop.

The driver dropped me off in front of a three-story building with a prominently displayed sign that read KRAMER'S MEAT MARKET above a large shop window. I was nearly sick from the emotional strain. I paid the driver and went inside. A few shoppers were present. When it was my turn, I asked the middle age woman who waited on me if I could speak with Leon Kramer.

"He doesn't work here anymore," she answered. A bucket of ice water poured over me could not have been more shocking. Of all the ifs, buts, and ands that I had chewed on during the last year, it had never occurred to me that he might have moved away. I needed to sit down, but there was no chair. I went outside, numb with disappointment and fear. Two doors down the street was a café where I could sit and think. Then I went back to the butchery and asked the woman if she knew where he went.

"No," she said, "but the boss should know."

"Can I talk to him?"

"He's out of town. He won't be back for another week." Oh God! I turned away to fight down the tears that were rising in my eyes. What now!

"Do you know if Leon Kramer has completed master?"

"Yes, he did," she said, then tended to a customer.

I left again, desperate to know what to do next. Maybe someone at the brother's home could tell me where I could find Leon. I went back to the café and asked for the phone book. I found Rudi Kramer's private number listed, and on a public telephone, inside the café, I dialed it. I hardly expected anyone to answer, yet someone did. When I heard a familiar voice my heart began to beat so hard that I feared it would burst. Tears choked my voice, "Leon? Is that you?"

"Yes it is." There was a little pause, then, sounding excited, "Stephanie, is that you?"

"Yes," I whispered. My legs were about to give way; I caught myself on a chair, still holding the phone in my hand.

"Where are you?"

"Here, in Munich, near your brother's butcher shop."

"Go to the shop, I'll be there right away," he said quickly and hung up.

I hurried back and waited in front of the door that leads to the apartments above. Suddenly, the door opened. I turned around, and there, in the doorway, stood Leon. For a moment, we just looked, silently taking each other in. An agonizing moment of fear, that I might have lost him, went by. Then he smiled, a beautifully contended smile, as if he had always known that I would come. He opened his arms and I rushed to him. The door fell shut, and the world went away.

"Oh, how I missed you," he said with a moan of agony. He buried his face on my shoulder as he held me tightly. "Why didn't you write?"

"I had some growing up to do," I whispered in his ear. He looked up and searched my eyes.

"And did you?" I just nodded.

And all the fear of having lost Leon, and the great joy of finding him again filled my eyes with tears. Leon kissed them away, gently, lovingly. And then he kissed me passionately, and I knew that we would always be together.